RUNNING TO THE HERO

HEROES OF FREEDOM RIDGE

HANNAH JO ABBOTT

"So if the Son sets you free, you will be free indeed."

— JOHN 8:36

Felicity Keaton looked over her shoulder as she picked up the flowing layers of tulle and lace and ran out the back door of the country club. No one was following her.

She whispered a word of thanks when she reached the back of the parking lot, glad that they had planned ahead and taken her car. Reaching in the purse she had slung over her shoulder, she grabbed her keys and clicked the button to open the trunk. There was the suitcase she had carefully packed for her two-week honeymoon. Next to it was another suitcase.

She reached in and lifted it out and set it in the parking spot.

"Goodbye, Clay," she said quietly. Hoping he would find the bag when he came looking for the car, she ran for the driver's side.

As she climbed in, she stuffed the layers of dress all around her. With her hands on the wheel, she took one deep breath and blew it out. This was the right thing to do, wasn't it?

She couldn't marry a man she didn't love, and after today, she knew for sure she didn't love him.

As she backed out of the parking spot, she reached for the veil that suddenly felt like a leash around her head. Removing it, she threw it in the back seat. It landed unceremoniously on the floor, signaling the end of her being a bride.

"I never really felt like a bride anyway," she said to herself. "All the parties, all the planning. It was never about me. It was all about them." She shook her head. "I should have ended it a long time ago." But she hadn't, and there was no use looking back. All she could do was look forward.

As she pulled onto the interstate, she wondered where forward was. They had booked a place for the honeymoon. Was it ridiculous to go there? What if Clay showed up? No, no, she couldn't do that. Clay had paid for it, and if he wanted to get away from the mess she had left him in, he could go there.

She would have to find her own place.

Wasn't it time for that anyway? Her parents had run her life for far too long. Now she needed to get away.

Oh, her parents.

What were they feeling now? Surely, by now her mom had found the note she had left in the bridal suite of the country club.

Clay, I'm sorry. I can't go through with it. This isn't right for me, and I think in time you'll find it's not right for you either - Felicity.

Her mom would be devastated. Her only daughter running away from the picture-perfect wedding she had planned, ruining all her dreams of this day. Her dad would be another story. He wouldn't be devastated, he would be angry. Felicity shivered slightly as she imagined the look on his face and the way he would clench his fists and shake them in the air. Felicity leaving his newest company vice president at the altar wouldn't hurt his feelings. It would hurt his reputation.

Once she was past the on-ramp of the interstate, she pressed the gas pedal down. What had she been thinking? She didn't even like the venue or the veil or the dress. She had tried on at least twenty dresses, and this was the one her mom begged her to choose. *Fine*, she had thought, *she cares more about it than I do.*

And her dad had cared more about Clay than she had. All the times she had thought there wasn't much chemistry between them came to mind. He never reached for her hand while they drove in the car or told her why he loved her. She had gone out with him at first because they were a good match. And at twenty-eight, maybe she should be more concerned about being compatible than about sparks flying between them.

The day her dad had hired him, Felicity had tried to quiet the butterflies banging around in her gut. She told herself it was excitement, but she got the sense that at that moment her future had been decided for her.

Now she knew she had overlooked a lot in the last several months, and when it came down to it, she just couldn't go through with it.

Felicity shook her head and checked the signs as she

drove. She really should think about a plan. A December wedding in Colorado in the snow and mountains had seemed like a dream. Now that it had turned into a nightmare, she would need someplace to stay. For how long, she didn't know. They were supposed to honeymoon for two weeks and head home in time for Christmas. So she had no commitments for the next few weeks.

She turned up the music to drown out her thoughts. She would drive until she found a decent hotel. She could stay the night and decide what to do in the morning.

Right now, these bobby pins had to come out of her hair. Holding the wheel with her knee, she started grabbing for pins and tossing them in the cupholder. Several of them missed and fell in between the crack in the seat. "Shoot," she said, taking her eyes off the road to dig her hand in the cushion.

When she looked back up, she gasped as a car pulled over right in front of her and slowed down. She slammed on the brakes and jerked the wheel, but squeezed her eyes closed, knowing it was too late.

DR. JUDE PALMER PULLED A PEN FROM HIS POCKET AND carefully checked the list on his clipboard. The hospital had switched to digital records a few years ago, and most doctors were used to carrying around an electronic tablet. Jude had to input everything later, but he liked to make notes of his patients in writing. No telling when the system could go down. He needed to have the information on hand at all times.

"Excuse me Dr. Palmer," his nurse said, walking into his office located in the back hall of the emergency room. "There's an accident victim coming in. They're five minutes out."

Jude nodded calmly, even as his heart began to pound wildly. Car accident victims always did that to him. "I'll be ready. Just let me know when they arrive."

The nurse nodded and turned to leave.

Jude used his index finger to push his black-rimmed glasses up from his nose. In his mind, he went over the steps of assessing the victim, careful to think of everything they would need to check. Turned out, he didn't need the nurse to come and tell him. He heard the commotion when the patient was moved into triage. That was one benefit of a small-town hospital. He could wait and let the nurses assess the victim first, but he was available and he didn't want to waste any time.

Down the hall, he stepped toward the curtain as the EMTs gave their report.

"Female. Twenty-eight. Car accident, hit the car in front of her, and then hit on the passenger side by a second car. According to witnesses, the car spun around and hit the wall on the driver's side. Cuts and scrapes, complains of wrist pain and head pain."

Jude carefully considered all of the information and prepared himself to see the woman. He furrowed his eyebrows as he saw a large pile of white fabric billowing onto the floor behind the curtain. What did you call that stuff? Not lace, but something like that. It was fluffy. Was that a wedding dress?

He cleared his throat and pulled back the curtain.

The woman sniffed as she looked up at him. Her long, dark hair went in all directions. It was as if it were halfway up and halfway down. Her cheeks were streaked with black mascara. It was indeed a wedding gown, which he was sure had been pure white. It was streaked with bright-red blood now.

"I'm Dr. Palmer." He reached for the chart that the nurse had started. "Mrs. Keaton," he read. "I'm sure you're feeling shaken, and a lot of things hurt, but can you tell me where the worst pain is?"

She nodded slightly as she spoke with a strain in her voice. "My wrist. And my head hurts."

"Did you hit your head?"

She put her hand to her forehead. "I don't think so, but I can't really remember."

"That's ok. We're going to give you a full check and make sure we don't miss anything."

She sniffed and pressed her lips together as she straightened up.

Jude glanced around. "Is your husband with you?"

She blinked as fresh tears filled her eyes. "No. I'm…I'm not married."

Jude raised his eyebrows but didn't say anything.

"I know this looks crazy. I was supposed to get married today. But it didn't happen."

A million questions came to his mind, but he snapped his mouth shut and nodded. He went to work checking her injuries. He didn't need to know her life story to take care of her health. Putting his stethoscope to his ears, he moved to listen to her heart and lungs. Everything sounded clear. He checked her pupils and reminded himself to focus on the medical aspects and not the beautiful golden-brown color.

"I'm going to check your wrist now. I'll be gentle, but it may be painful."

She blinked rapidly, but nodded and held out her arm.

It didn't look misshapen or bent. That was a good sign. At least it didn't appear to be a complete break. She winced as he gingerly gripped her arm and moved her wrist in a circle.

"I would like to get an x-ray. It's likely just a sprain, but we can't rule out a break without taking a look."

"Okay," she said, her voice just above a whisper.

He looked her in the eyes then. She was like a sad kitten who wanted to cower in the corner. But she was trying to be brave.

He didn't usually do this, but he couldn't help it. He reached out and patted her on the shoulder. "Everything is going to be all right." When her eyes met his, he silently prayed it was true.

2

*H*airline fracture. Felicity kept running the words over and over again in her mind. She was supposed to be on her honeymoon. This was supposed to be the happiest time of her life. Instead she was in a town that she didn't know, with no one that she knew, with a crushed car and a splint on her wrist. At least it wasn't a cast. She could take the splint off to shower and wash her hands. She would have to be careful with the stitches on her other arm. The accident had happened so fast, she couldn't remember, but she must have used her arm to shield her face from the window glass breaking. Dr. Palmer had said he could put a cast on her wrist, but since the fracture was so small, he felt comfortable with the splint.

Dr. Palmer. Felicity couldn't explain it. He had barely said two words to her during the entire examination, and yet there was something about him. He stepped into the room and she immediately felt a little bit better. She'd never had a doctor that was that good looking. His dark hair was set off by the thick frames of his glasses. When he looked her in the eye, it was as if he knew exactly how she was feeling in that moment. But how could he? He must just be very good at his job. After all, as an ER doctor, she was sure he saw plenty of accident victims.

She sat on the exam table waiting for her discharge papers. Her wedding gown was balled up in a hospital garbage bag. How appropriate. A nurse had found her some scrubs to wear so she didn't have to walk around in the white frilly outfit. The nurse had also managed to find her a ponytail holder to tie up her wild mane.

"But what am I going to do now?" she asked herself out loud. "I don't even know where to go." So far all she had seen of the town was the inside of the ambulance and the hospital. She didn't even know if there was a decent hotel nearby.

The nurse bustled back into the room carrying a clipboard and a pen. "How long are you in town for?" she asked.

Felicity shrugged and her eyes grew wide at the reminder that she had no idea what her plans were for the foreseeable future.

The nurse gave her a kind smile. "It's all right. I'm only asking because Dr. Palmer wants you to follow up with an orthopedic doctor. We can help you set something up in town if you're going to be here for a while. Or you can find your own doctor back home."

"I… I'm not sure. I didn't really plan to be here in the first place."

The nurse gave her a concerned look. "Do you have a place to stay?"

Felicity shook her head. "Is there a good hotel nearby? And can I call an Uber?"

"Oh sure. Freedom has lots of good hotels. Of course, the nicest place is the resort. You might be able to get a room, but they are pretty booked up this time of year, with the holidays and all."

Felicity quietly repeated the words "the resort."

"Oh yes, lots of people travel to Freedom just to come to Freedom Ridge Resort for the holiday season. There's skiing and restaurants and all kinds of entertainment."

"That does sound nice. But I don't know how long I'll be staying," Felicity said.

The nurse nodded. "Sure, sure, I understand. But if you do happen to stay in town, there's lots of Christmas events coming up. There's nothing like Christmas in Freedom."

"Thanks, I'll keep that in mind."

"Well I've got your discharge papers here." The nurse read over the directions, and Felicity tried to listen, but everything was overwhelming. "If you'll just sign this"—the nurse pointed at the clipboard—"then you'll be out of here."

Felicity took the clipboard and signed the papers. She gave a kind of half smile, trying to convince herself that everything was going to be all right. She scooted herself off the table using only her good hand and gathered her purse, whispering a prayer of thanks that it had survived the wreck. She had no idea what she would do about her car. The paramedics had slipped a card in her purse for the name of the wrecker company that came to tow it to a garage, but she would have to worry about that later.

Right now, all she needed was a place to stay for the night and a shower to try and wash away this horrible day.

When she opened the door to walk out, she only made one step before she collided with something. "Ooof," she said, instinctively reaching to cradle her wrist.

"Oh, I'm so sorry. I didn't mean to… I, umm…" Dr. Palmer stuttered and straightened his glasses as he stared at Felicity.

"It's all right. I'm okay. I'm okay." Felicity repeated the phrase, trying to convince herself.

"I couldn't help but overhear that you didn't plan to be in town here. And I can tell from the events of the day this wasn't exactly your plan."

Felicity shook her head. How much should she tell the stranger? "No, this was not my plan for the day. But I'll figure it out."

Dr. Palmer seemed to fumble in his pocket. His eyes darted from the floor to the ceiling and back and forth again as if he wasn't sure if he should say what he wanted to say. Finally, he must've decided to go ahead. "Here's my card." He quickly pressed a piece of paper into Felicity's hand. "I don't want to make you uncomfortable, but if you need to find a doctor to see while you're here, or if you need anything else, please let me know." Without another word, he turned and walked the other direction, disappearing around the corner.

Felicity stared after him, wondering what kind of person he was. He was a doctor, after all, so he must care about people. But did he often offer his card and phone number to women he didn't know?

She shook her head and told herself not to think about

it anymore. She didn't have time to wonder about him when she needed to get on with her life. She'd had enough of men for the foreseeable future. She reached in her purse for her phone and opened the app to order a car. Within a few minutes, she sat outside the Martin County Veterans' Memorial Hospital. When the black sedan pulled up and she climbed in, clinging to her purse and suitcase, she didn't miss a minute before telling the driver, "Please take me to the Freedom Ridge Resort."

Felicity watched out the window as they drove through the town. If she had been on vacation instead of stranded, it would have been a beautiful place to be. They must've had fresh snow recently because the ground was covered in white. They drove through the main part of the small town, and she could imagine tourists walking in and out of the shops on Main Street. What would it be like to be here for fun?

Then she had another thought. What if she decided to make this fun? When had she been on a fun vacation? Sure, her parents took her plenty of places as a teenager, but they were usually part of a business trip or something educational. Since college she had become serious and focused on her studies and then her job. Maybe that's what had landed her in the position she found herself in. She'd been too busy to have fun, make friends, date boys.

Maybe that's why when Clay asked her out she didn't think she needed to look for better options. No, there hadn't been a lot of spark with him, but then again, maybe that wasn't real life. Her parents had an amiable marriage, but Felicity couldn't really say that she thought they were in love. In love? What was that anyway? Maybe that was just something that happened in movies and books and not in real life. Not in her life anyway.

Now was her chance. She was supposed to be on a honeymoon for two weeks. What if this became her own vacation? Her own break from her serious, busy life? With a nod at the decision, Felicity straightened up in her seat. Christmas in Freedom. That sounded fun. What if she could be fun? She could stroll up and down the streets. Maybe she wouldn't go snow skiing or hiking in cold weather, but she could have a good time.

Yes, that was it. She would celebrate Christmas in Freedom. And just maybe she would celebrate her freedom at Christmas.

3

*J*ude carefully parked his car in the garage, then climbed the steps up to his two-story cabin. He put his keys on the hook by the door and flipped on the light switch. A quick glance about the room told him that everything was exactly as he had left it.

He thought for the hundredth time that the house was much too big for himself. But it was only him, and it would always be only him. His mother frequently suggested that he get a cat or a dog, but why would he want to leave a pet at home alone all day? Or the odd hours of night that he had to work shifts at the ER? No, this was his life. Alone.

Moving into the kitchen, he reached in for the glass dish containing one of the meals he had prepared earlier in the week. Each one was carefully labeled with the day of the week. He reached for Saturday and turned on the oven to preheat. It was nice that he had found a website with recipes for one. He enjoyed cooking, especially since it was so different than being an ER doctor. There was no way to kill a zucchini or a carrot.

His thoughts drifted to the woman he helped in the wedding dress that day. Felicity. He usually remembered the names of his patients; that photographic memory was hard to shake. But this was different. There was something about her. It wasn't just that she was an accident victim, although those usually stuck in his mind more than other patients. No, it was the look in her eyes that said she needed something.

He shook his head. No, she didn't need him. No one needed him. Well, maybe they needed him as their doctor, but not as anything else.

He absentmindedly flipped on the television and turned to the news as he waited for his dinner to be ready. Not that there was much news to keep up with in Freedom, Colorado. But that wouldn't be on TV anyway. The news in Freedom came in coffee shops and church pews and women's sewing circles. He assumed about the sewing circles, since he'd never actually attended one of those. Coffee shops he generally avoided—there was too much small talk, and he wasn't good at small talk. He did attend church. His mother would just die if he didn't. He still believed in God and tried to be a good person. How could he not be a good person? He saved lives in the ER every day.

But did that really mean he had to know whose sister's dog had puppies that week or whose neighbor broke up with her boyfriend or who got a new job?

In the town of Freedom, unfortunately, it did. That's what came with living in a small town.

He'd been looking for a place to do his residency when his grandmother passed away, leaving him the mountain cabin. She had used it for vacations and for renting out as a side income. But Jude jumped at the chance to live in seclusion away from the world. Or so he thought. Who would've known living in a secluded mountain cabin in a small town would mean that everyone needed to know everything about you? He didn't need to know anyone's story to help them. He only needed to know their symptoms or their injuries and their medical history. The rest was too personal and too personal got you in trouble.

Speaking of too personal, he probably should call his mom. It was about time for their weekly chat. Picking up his phone, he knew that the oven timer would beep before long and give him an opportunity to cut off the call. After two rings, she picked up just like always. "Hello?"

"Hi, Mom, it's me," he said as if she didn't have caller ID.

"Hi, honey, how was your day?" She asked the same question that she always asked to begin their conversations.

Jude found it comforting to know that she was always there, always asking the same question. Even if he knew exactly what the next question was going to be. "It was fine. Mom. How was your day?"

"Just fine. Did you meet anyone new today?"

"I met patients," Jude gave his usual reply.

"No, I mean did you meet *anyone*?" She emphasized the last word.

Of course, his mom wished that he would be married and

have a family. And he knew it was because she loved being married to his dad and raising him and his brother. He swallowed hard and tried to push away the thought of his sibling.

"No, Mom, I didn't meet a woman." That wasn't true. He had met a woman. But she was a patient and most likely he wasn't going to see her again. Most likely. Despite the fact that he had given her his phone number. Why in the world did he do that? He had never done that before. No wonder he couldn't get Felicity off his mind. But it wasn't because of her; it was because of him. He had done something dumb. He would have to remember never to do that again.

Jude fumbled about the kitchen, waiting for his dinner to be ready, and halfheartedly listened to his mom go on about her friend group. One woman was in the hospital, one friend had a daughter who was going through a divorce. There was a never ending list of troubles among the people that she knew.

"But of course I guess I can't complain. Even if my son lives three states away and never visits."

"I've told you, Mom, my work is my life. I can't just pick up and leave. But you are welcome to visit me anytime. I have plenty of room, and you would enjoy it here. Freedom is a tourist destination you know."

"Oh I know, I know. You've said so before. And I've been there, remember? I visited your grandmother one Christmas. But that's a vacation. That's not visiting my son"

Jude sighed. "I'm sorry, Mom. Maybe next year." The timer on the oven beeped then, rescuing him from the same old conversation. "Mom, that's my dinner, it's ready. I'll have to let you go."

"All right. I hope that you're eating well and taking care of yourself. I've heard stories about ER doctors who live off of caffeine and fast food."

"I think you know me better than that. But I can assure you I do not eat fast food." He didn't mention anything about the caffeine.

"Good-bye, son. I love you."

"I love you too, Mom. Bye."

Jude took his dinner out of the oven and prepared his plate. As he carried it to the kitchen table to sit and eat, he silently thanked God for the food.

He swallowed hard as he thought of it, but he couldn't help whispering a prayer for the woman in the wedding dress.

4

Felicity looked up, down, left and right, trying to take in the grandeur of the resort all at once. Had there ever been this many Christmas decorations in one building at the same time? Everywhere she looked was covered in greenery or red ribbons or lights. They hadn't missed a spot.

Slowly, she moved toward the welcome desk and away from the chill of the outside.

"Welcome to Freedom Ridge Resort," the woman behind the desk said with a wide smile.

"Hi," Felicity said. She wasn't sure what to say after that. The truth was, she had never checked into a hotel on her own. Her father had always handled that sort of thing. It really was time she grew up. "Um, I wanted to see if you have a room available."

"Of course. Let me see. We are pretty busy this week, but we've had a few cancellations. What size room?"

Felicity bit her lip. "Just for one."

"Perfect, let me see here. Yes, we have a few rooms available. How long will you be staying with us?"

Felicity's stomach churned at the question. "I'm not sure, honestly. Let's say five nights." That would work. By then she could come up with a plan.

"We have a queen room with a view of the slopes. How does that sound?"

"Perfect."

"All right. I'll just need a little information and a credit card for the reservation."

Felicity answered all the questions and reached to pull a credit card from her purse. It carried her name, but the bill went to her father. She would take care of that soon, but for now, she had no choice but to let him pay for her unexpected vacation.

The woman swiped the card and handed it back to Felicity, then handed her a folder with a room key. "You're in room 424. Here is a list of amenities for you. We have several restaurants, as well as a spa and a gift shop. So if you're interested in any of that, all the information is here in the brochure. But if you have any other questions, please feel free to give us a call and we're always happy to help twenty-four hours a day."

Felicity slowly nodded as she took the information. What would she do with her days completely free and no one to tell her anything to do or anywhere to be?

The woman behind the desk smiled as she pointed. "The elevators are this way, and that will take you up to your floor. Enjoy your stay."

"Thank you," Felicity said. As she turned to go, she reached for her rolling suitcase. It had almost been left in the accident, but somehow she'd had the presence of mind as the EMTs carried her to the ambulance to yell out, "My suitcase! It's in the trunk!" One of the men turned and retrieved it. The only thing worse than being alone in a strange town without her car would be being alone without any clothes.

Felicity made her way toward the elevator. Once up on the fourth floor and in front of room 424, she opened the door and gasped at the cozy room. "This is perfect," she practically squealed. She shut the door behind her before making a running leap onto the bed. If she wasn't going to be on a honeymoon with a husband, she might as well enjoy a winter retreat as a single woman.

Except that this room must be expensive. She'd never had to think about that before. But her parents had just paid for a wedding that she ran from, and they wouldn't be happy about paying for this trip. Even if the charges wouldn't make a dent in their bank account.

Felicity sighed thinking about all the things she'd left behind. Her family, her job at her dad's company, the only life she knew. She would have to figure out a way to make it up to them, or she would have to think about how to start a new life.

For now, all she could think about was getting a hot tray from room service and soaking in a long bath in that luxurious tub. Tomorrow, she would think about a plan.

Tomorrow, she would start a new day as her own person. Felicity Keaton, independent woman.

Now she only had to decide what she wanted to do for the rest of her life.

5

elicity stepped out of the Freedom Ridge Resort the next morning into the brisk winter air. She hoped the pair of dark jeans and sweater would keep her warm enough under the thick winter coat.

Today she would experience Freedom—both the city and the feeling. No Mom, no Dad, no Clay, no one to boss her around or give her an agenda. She could do whatever she wanted. Right now what she wanted was to find a bakery with coffee and breakfast.

She had ordered a car to pick her up, and she watched as it pulled up under the awning in front of the resort. She had gotten a call from the mechanic where the police had her car towed. They said it would be at least a week before she could get it back. "I guess I'll be here at least a week then," she had said. That didn't sound too bad.

It was only a few minutes' drive to the main part of town. The driver had given her a suggestion for a place to get breakfast and dropped her off right in front of the shop. Felicity looked around as she stepped out of the car and shut the door behind her. What a quaint little place this was. The shops looked like somewhere she could wander around for a couple of hours at least.

The sign over the door read Stories and Scones. It sounded like a perfectly adorable place to get coffee in the perfect little tourist town. A bell rang overhead as she opened the door and walked inside. She made her way to the counter and looked up at the menu. She knew immediately that she would have to try the seasonal special: peppermint mocha coffee. She took a deep breath and the scent of cinnamon and vanilla and something else…was it orange? Whatever it was, it smelled delicious, and her stomach growled right on cue.

The woman behind the counter stepped up and smiled at her. "Good morning. What can I get for you?"

Felicity returned the smile, determined that she was going to have a happy day. "I'd like a peppermint mocha coffee, and I'll take your suggestion on your most popular croissant. I've heard this is the best place in town to get breakfast."

The woman laughed. "Well, I don't know about the best place. We have a lot of great places to eat here, but I'm thrilled that someone recommended it. And because we only have it for a limited time, I would suggest the cinnamon cream cheese croissant."

"Perfect. I'll take one of those."

As the woman rang up the order, she looked up and gave Felicity a glance. "Are you visiting town?"

"Yes, I am. I just got in last night."

"Wonderful! How long are you staying?"

Felicity bit her lip at the question she didn't have an answer for. "I'm not actually sure. Maybe a couple weeks."

The woman gave her a curious look. "Oh? What brings you to town?"

Felicity wondered how many times she would answer this question. Did everyone in town want to know your story the first moment they met you?

"Well, actually, I wasn't planning to be here. I was driving through when I had an accident."

"Oh, you poor thing!" The woman reached out and patted her hand. "Are you all right? Do you need anything?"

Felicity stared at her and tilted her head. That was an unexpected question. Were all strangers in town this nice? At the moment, it occurred to her that she might need something. Her car was in the shop, and she didn't know when it was going to be finished or how much it was going to cost. And she couldn't live off her dad's credit card forever. Before she could finish the thought, she heard herself blurt out, "I need a job." Had she actually just said that? It was true, she probably did need to make some money. Especially if she didn't know how long she would be here. But she hadn't meant to say it to a perfect stranger.

The woman tilted her head as if in thought. "Hmm. Well now, I'm not hiring here. I think I have all the holiday help I need. But a lot of places usually hire this month. I'll keep my ears open for anything. What's your name, dear?"

"Felicity. Felicity Keaton."

"Felicity, I'm Jan. Why don't you leave me your number, and if I hear of something, I'll let you know."

Felicity stepped back in surprise. "You would do that?"

"Of course, we like to help people out around here," Jan said, as if Felicity were already part of the community.

"But you don't even know me."

"Are you a criminal?" Jan asked.

"No," Felicity answered, cracking a smile.

"Do you need a job?"

"Yes."

"Well then, I know everyone who owns businesses here. If I hear of someone looking to hire, I'll let you know. Then they can decide for themself if they want to give you a shot."

"Thank you, thank you very much." Felicity moved aside as another customer came in to order. She waited for her coffee and croissant, and when Jan handed it to her with a smile, somehow she felt a little bit better. No one had been that kind to her. Her own parents had treated her like an employee that they got to boss around more than a friend or a daughter.

Out on the sidewalk, she tightened her coat around her as she shivered. It wasn't this cold in December in Texas, where she had lived her whole life. How had she ever been talked into a winter destination wedding in Colorado? She would have said no, if it wasn't for the fact that her parents had been married at the same lodge and it was her mother's dream. Her dad and Clay had been so excited to welcome guests to a winter wonderland at the ceremony. She hoped they enjoyed their time. They were certainly happier together than she and Clay ever had been.

Still, the snow was pretty, as long as it didn't block her in or cause some kind of danger. And as long as she didn't slip walking on the sidewalk.

There were a number of shops on Main Street, and she was sure she could spend the entire day shopping. But with her new resolve to make her own way financially, maybe she should stick with window shopping.

Felicity wandered down the sidewalk, peering in the windows. One sign in particular caught her eye. Wick and Sarcasm. What an interesting name. She swung the door open and stepped inside. A myriad of smells greeted her. Cinnamon, vanilla, spice, mint. She looked around at the rows of candles on shelves. Oh, of course, wick because it's a candle shop. She peered at the titles on some of the candles, and the sarcasm part started to make sense. The shelves were lined with candles with names like "laundry day," "Caffeinated Pumpkin," and "Book Boyfriend."

"Hey there," a girl said, coming from the back room that was separated from the counter by a curtain. "Can I help you find anything?"

"I'm just looking around."

"Help yourself. We have a special, if you buy three candles." The girl pointed to the sign. "We have some Christmas candles available for a limited time too. Just let me know if you need anything."

Felicity nodded and continued walking around the store. The phone rang, and the woman moved to answer it. "Wick and Sarcasm. Oh hi. Yes, we do special orders, but right now I need you to give me at least a week to get them ready. We're in our busy season and I'm way behind. Okay, sure, twelve of those? You got it. I'll have them next week, and I'll call you if they're done before then."

Felicity's ears perked up as she listened to the woman talk. She didn't mean to eavesdrop, but then again, she didn't seem to be keeping it quiet.

When she hung up the phone, Felicity spoke up. "You're pretty busy, huh?" she asked, trying to sound casual.

"You have no idea. I usually have a couple of college students who are home on break at Christmas that help me, but all of them decided to go out of town this year instead."

Felicity approached the counter, feeling brave. "So are you looking for some help?"

The woman raised her eyebrows. "Yes, I am. If I find the right person. I can't make candles in the back and be out here to answer the phone and help customers. We're slow at the moment, but there are times I have five people waiting in line. Are you looking for a job?"

Felicity nodded. "Yes, I am. But I feel like I should be honest. I just got into town, and I don't know exactly how long I'll be here. At least until Christmas, but after that, I don't know."

The woman nodded and bit her lip. "Well, this is our busiest time of year, and we are pretty desperate. So if you can be here until Christmas, I could use the help. After that we can see what happens. How does that sound?"

"That would be wonderful. I also should probably tell you that I've never worked in a store before."

The woman laughed. "You've never interviewed for a job, have you?"

Felicity felt her cheeks flush pink. "No."

"I think you're supposed to try to convince me to give you the job, not talk me out of it."

"I know. I just don't want you to think I tricked you into hiring me." Just the thought made her stomach turn. "I want to be honest. I don't know anything about this kind of job, but I will do my best, and I'm a fast learner. If you give me a chance, I'll show up when I'm supposed to and I'll work hard." That was the best she could offer.

The woman crossed her arms and smiled. "Well, I've had employees that didn't even do that. So I'll be happy to give you a chance. Honestly, any help would be great at this point." She held out a hand across the counter. "I'm Ashley, by the way."

Felicity reached out to shake her hand. "Felicity."

She gave an amount per hour, and Felicity nodded.

"That's reasonable. When do you want me to start?"

"How about right now? I can show you how to work the register and give you a rundown of the prices. Then we can troubleshoot before we get busy today."

"Sounds good," Felicity said.

"Perfect. Come on, you can put your coat and purse in the back. I'll get you an apron and give you a crash course in running the front counter. I'll be here, but I've already got Christmas orders to fill, and I need to be working."

Felicity hurried to the back and put her purse and coat on a hook. Back out front, she took the apron Ashley handed her and then gave every ounce of her attention as Ashley explained the cash register. It felt like an eternity as she explained the different types of candles and how to input the price.

"The candles should all be labeled on the bottom, but if you find a missing one, there's a list of the sizes and prices."

Felicity nodded. She had promised to work hard, but already her head was spinning.

Ashley seemed to sense her nervousness and patted her on the shoulder. "I know it's a lot. Trust me, the best way to learn is just to start. You'll get more familiar as you go along. It will be fine."

Just then the door opened, signaling that Felicity was about to get her first chance at the job. She pasted on a smile as she looked up.

"Do you think you're ready to handle this?" Ashley asked.

Felicity took a deep breath. "I'm ready to try."

"Wonderful. I've got a long list to get to in the back. But let me know if you need me."

"I will," Felicity said. But Ashley had already hurried through the door. She was like a busy bee flitting around to all her tasks. What was it like to own and run your own business? Sure, there was a lot of responsibility, but it must be nice to be your own boss. Felicity felt as if she hadn't even been the own boss of her life. But it was time for that to change.

Even if it meant working behind the counter of a candle shop where she felt completely lost.

Jude scowled as he walked into Wick and Sarcasm. How in the world he had been assigned this task, he didn't know. Did the emergency room staff really need a Christmas party, and were candles really the best gift? Wasn't that a major cause of house fires this time of year?

Jude shuddered. He had seen enough burn victims this year already. Particularly on Thanksgiving when everyone decided to become a master chef for one day of the year when they'd never even cooked before.

He shook his head as he moved toward the counter, a movement to his left caught his eye and he turned that way.

"I'll be right with you." The woman looked at him and recognition dawned. "Oh hey."

"Hey," Jude said, recognizing Felicity Keaton right away. He immediately looked to her right arm where she held a box full of candles that looked rather heavy. Instinctively, he reached out and took the box from her. "You're not supposed to be bearing that much weight on your arm," he said.

"Oh, right." Felicity looked away sheepishly. "It doesn't hurt really, if I keep it flat."

"I'm glad, but if it's going to heal properly, you need to let it rest."

"Okay. You can set it on the floor. I'll just lift the candles out one at a time. With my other hand."

He looked at her as if seeing her there for the first time. She wore a bright-red apron with the Wick and Sarcasm logo on the front. "You work here?" he asked.

She nodded.

"I didn't think you were from around here." Why did

he say that? He didn't know where she was from. He didn't keep up with people in town. She could have lived here for years and he wouldn't know. He just assumed.

"Oh, well, I'm not from here. I don't even know how long I'll be in town. But I'm here for now, and I needed a job, and Ashley needed help." She turned her palm to the ceiling and shrugged. "So here I am."

"Oh," Jude heard himself say. What else should he say after that? What kind of person ended up in a town by mistake and decided to stay and get a job? Jude had planned his life years in advance, from the time he was seven.

Felicity cleared her throat. "What can I help you with?"

"Oh, right." He was there for a reason. He didn't wander into shops in town to window shop. "I'm here to pick up an order."

"Sure, let me check with Ashley."

"It's under the hospital's name. Or maybe Susan? I'm not sure." He wondered again why he had agreed to this. They only asked because he had to drive past the shop on his way to work.

"No problem. Ashley probably knows."

Jude fell silent again as Felicity walked to the back. She was curiouser at every turn. What was it about her that made him want to know her story? He treated dozens of patients every day, and he remembered most of them. But he didn't wonder about their lives and who they were beyond their treatment. She was a mystery though. Was she left at the altar, or did she do the leaving? Did she have a family that wondered where she was and that she would go back to? Or would she start a new life here and never look back?

He put the thoughts out of his head as she brought out the order, thankfully carrying it with her good arm. He didn't meet her eyes as she rang it up.

A little while later, Jude walked into the staff door of the hospital carrying the heavy box of candles. Susan had told him to put them in the cabinet in the break room and try not to let anyone see them. When he walked into the room, he saw balloons. He racked his brain trying to remember if there was a special event. Was he too busy to remember someone's birthday? His brain was filled with facts and procedures and the memory of so many patients, but he wasn't great at remembering to pay attention to the people he worked with.

He would say the people in his life, but to tell the truth, his coworkers were about the only people in his life. Besides his weekly call to his mother, he could go for days not talking to anyone besides his nurse and his patients.

Was he doing this all wrong? He had moved to Colorado for the peace and quiet—at least when he wasn't working. But had he taken it too far?

He put the box away in the cabinet and then turned to the table. Glancing at the "Happy Birthday Veronica" written on the cake, he made a mental note to tell her happy birthday. Maybe it was time to start paying attention to life going on around him.

6

Jude drank coffee at home. Black coffee from his French press. So why in the world was he walking into a frilly coffee shop on a Monday morning? He told himself it was ridiculous. You didn't just start being part of a town again by walking into a coffee shop and saying hello to people. But he'd heard that this was a popular place, and wasn't that where people got town news? Places like coffee shops and candle stores.

Not that he was going to Wick and Sarcasm today. He wasn't trying to see her; he was just trying to be nicer to people in general. It didn't have anything to do with the woman with dark hair that cascaded all the way down her back and eyes that told him she had been hurt. Not the hurt that meant she needed to go to the ER, but hurt deep down.

He heard the bell jingle over the door and walked in, hoping they served black coffee here.

"Anyway, thank you again. I might have wandered

around town all day too scared to ask for what I needed, but instead I started work."

Jude stopped in his tracks. How was her voice already so familiar?

Felicity turned. "Oh hey," she said, as if they were already old friends.

He cleared his throat. "Morning," he said.

"Good morning," Felicity said. She looked back at Jan behind the counter and lifted the coffee cup she held. "I'll get out of the way. See you later."

"You're never in the way here," Jan said. "Feel free to stay awhile. Browse the books if you have time."

Felicity nodded and stepped out of the way and gave him a quick smile as she moved toward the bookshelves.

Jude stepped to the counter.

"Good morning," Jan said. "What can I get for you?"

"Medium coffee, black," he said.

When Jan raised an eyebrow at him, he glanced at the items in the case. "And, um, a blueberry scone."

Jan smiled. "Coming right up."

Felicity came back to the counter with a piece of paper in her hand. "This looks fun!" she said brightly. "Is it a fundraiser?"

Jan glanced at the paper. "Oh the gingerbread house competition? Yes, the town council is hosting it to raise money for a new playground."

"That's wonderful. Can anyone sign up?" Felicity asked. Jude couldn't help but notice how her eyes danced in excitement.

"Sure can, but you're supposed to have two people to a team."

"Oh." Felicity's face fell. "I don't know anyone to sign up with."

Jan's eyes flashed, and Jude felt his stomach flip.

"Why don't you ask Jude?" Jan said, smiling.

"Dr. Palmer?" Felicity's voice showed her shock. She blinked rapidly and almost seemed like she was going to say no. Then she flashed a nervous smile, as if pulling together all her determination. "Sure, why not? Dr. Palmer, are you already signed up for the gingerbread house competition?"

He scoffed before he could stop himself. "No, I'm not."

"Would you like to be a team with me?"

"I um, well, I..." His words hung in the air and he wasn't sure what to say.

Jan must have sensed his awkwardness and tried to rescue him. "Oh, I was just kidding. He's always too busy for these kinds of things. You know he works a lot at the hospital."

"Right, I'm sorry. Of course, it's fine if you don't," Felicity said. She met his eyes and they flashed with a challenge. "I only thought it would be fun, and a nice way to support the town."

Jude swallowed hard to clear the lump forming in his throat. "I'll do it," he heard himself burst out.

Felicity stepped back as if in surprise. "Great!" She clapped her hands together. "Oh this will be fun, I've got some great ideas already. We'll have to get together to make a plan."

"Um, sure. You have my number on the card I gave you, right?"

"Oh yes, I do."

"Great, just text me and we'll set up a time." He reached for the coffee cup and white paper sack that Jan held out. "See you," he said before rushing out the door.

Out on the sidewalk, he took a deep breath of cold air. Had he really just agreed to do a Christmas town competition with a woman he didn't even know? How long had he been avoiding these kinds of events? They seemed silly and frivolous compared to working in the ER where people really needed him.

A little nudge inside told him the town needed him too. And he had seen Felicity's eyes. He didn't know what she was looking for, but he knew she needed help. It couldn't be a coincidence that he kept running into her. Maybe he was just supposed to be there and see what happened. That was different. He was used to having everything figured out. Ever since he was a kid, he had known what he wanted to be.

Then again, maybe a little mystery in his life could be a good thing.

7

*J*ude stepped into Stories and Scones for the second time in one week. Which was funny, since he had probably been inside it only twice in the whole time he had lived there up to this point.

He didn't have to wait long, since Felicity was already sitting at a small round table in the corner.

"Hey," she called out, waving as if she needed to let him know where she was. "Are you ready for this?"

Jude wasn't sure there was anything in the world he was less prepared for. "I'm here," he said.

"Well, that's a start." Felicity giggled. "I've been looking at pictures and printed a few things off to show you. But we'll have to figure out how to actually build it."

"Okay." Jude took his messenger bag from his shoulder and carefully set it on the floor as he took a seat. "What do you have in mind?"

"The theme of the competition is 'Hometown Christmas.' So I don't want it to be just any place, but something that really feels like it fits in Freedom. I thought I'd see what you think, since it's your hometown."

Jude crossed his arms and leaned back in the chair. Was that true? He'd never actually thought of Freedom as his hometown.

When he didn't respond, Felicity spoke up again. "How long have you lived here anyway? Did you grow up here?"

"No, I moved here a few years ago, when I started my fellowship at the hospital. I had considered several locations, but my grandmother left me the house that she used as a rental property. I decided to move here and live in the house while I paid off student loans."

Felicity nodded. "That makes sense. Where did you grow up?"

"Kentucky," he said.

"Really?" Her eyebrows shot up as she leaned back in her seat.

"Is that surprising?"

Felicity shrugged. "Just different than Colorado. I've never thought about picking up and moving states away from where I grew up."

"You just moved here."

Felicity blinked rapidly as she leaned on her elbows on the table. "I don't know if I would say that I've moved here. I'm here for now, and it wasn't something I planned." She spoke with a low voice, even though there was no one else to hear.

"Oh, I'm, uh, I'm sorry. I didn't mean to bring up personal matters."

Felicity looked at him. "It's all right. You're one of the few people who know that I showed up here in my wedding dress. I guess it's not a secret, just not something I've talked about."

"Do you…uh, want to talk about it?"

She tilted her chin up and blew out a breath. "I left my own wedding. I ran away in my wedding dress. I just couldn't go through with it."

"Oh." He dropped his eyes to the table and swallowed to give himself time to think of something to say. "I can't imagine what that felt like."

"Yeah, I hope not. I wouldn't wish it on anyone." She paused for a minute. "But honestly, I know it was the right decision. Running from my wedding is bad, but it was better to tell him now than to regret it for the rest of my life."

"What did he do to you?" Jude tightened his fist, wanting to know if he had hurt her.

She sighed. "He's not a bad guy, but I didn't love him, and I'm sure he didn't love me. He loved the idea of being married to me, but not me. Really everything started with my dad." She shivered. "I should have known from the first day. He knew who my dad was and was asking me questions about the company."

"So he was trying to use you?" Jude furrowed his eyebrows in confusion.

Felicity nodded. "He wanted to work for my dad. So he waited until we had been dating a few weeks to say he wanted to meet my dad. After that, he spent more time talking to Dad than he did to me. But by then they were planning the future of the company together, and I was just part of the bargain."

A sour taste filled Jude's mouth. He wanted to throw

up at the thought of someone using her for a position at a company. "I don't know much about business, but that's terrible."

"Mmhmm."

"Did he actually need to marry you to get the job?" Jude asked.

"No. That part hurts. Now they can have what they wanted together, and I'll be the one pushed aside. Clay would have married me still. He wanted a corporate wife who would take care of his house and plan office Christmas parties. But there was never a spark between us. He told me that was fine, we could have a platonic marriage."

Jude pushed back, grimacing in disgust. "Platonic marriage? What's that?"

Felicity shrugged. "Not a real marriage I guess. More like a business partnership, which is what the whole thing turned out to be."

Jude took a deep breath and leaned in. "Wow. I'm sorry. I had no idea. So you decided to move to Freedom that day?"

"I didn't decide anything. I just left. And then I had an accident and ended up here. I don't really know what's next for me. But for now, I'm here, and I want to enjoy Christmas. A real hometown Christmas. Not the Christmas of the corporate world I grew up in." She patted the table. "And now I would like to plan how we're going to win this gingerbread house competition."

Jude smiled. He wanted to ask her more questions, but he waved a hand as if pushing it away. "All right, tell me what you're wanting to do."

"I'm staying at the resort, so of course, that was my first thought. But I think that actually says more about people coming to visit the town. Now that I've been here a few days, I see that people who really live here and work here congregate on Main Street. The owners of the shops all know each other and help each other. Yesterday, Jan needed help bringing in boxes of Christmas coffee cups that were delivered, and the owner of Freedom Fudge Factory went down to carry them with his son-in-law. It's just nice that they know each other and help each other without asking for something in return."

"That is nice," Jude said. He rubbed his chin, thinking.

"Have you noticed that in the town?"

He sighed. "Honestly, I guess I've been too busy to notice."

"What do you mean? You don't get involved much in town?"

"That's one way to put it. I don't know. When I moved here, I was just trying to make it with my crazy schedule at the hospital. And if I wasn't working, I only had time to eat and sleep and go back to work."

"You didn't stop in for coffee or eat out? I feel like I've met ten people just walking down the street."

Jude squirmed in his seat. "No, I eat at home. It's healthier." He shrugged. "I go to church on Sundays, but I'll admit I come in at the last minute and I leave when it's over."

Felicity tapped her chin with her index finger. "Do you not like people?"

"Of course, I like people. I spend all day working with people."

Felicity nodded slowly. "You know, before I came here, I thought I knew a lot of people. Goodness, we invited two hundred of them to my wedding, and that was cutting the list down significantly. But I found out I didn't really know them. They were business associates of my dad, or acquaintances who probably only spent time with us because of my dad's money. No one has called to make sure I'm okay. They don't actually care about me because we're not friends. But you have something better than that here. People really care about each other." She gave him a serious look. "If I were you, I wouldn't take that for granted."

Jude stared at her, the truth hitting him square in the chest. "You might be right about that."

8

Wednesday evening, Felicity stood in the parking lot of Freedom Bible Church and blew into her hands that felt like ice cubes. The mid-week hymns and prayers service felt like and easy entry into the community. She couldn't remember the last time she had been to church. Maybe some Christmas Eve service years ago. Probably before her grandmother died. After that, her dad didn't see the point of it. Mom probably would have liked to go, at least for holidays, but she wasn't going to stand up to Dad.

Anyway, here she was. If she was going to change who she was, might as well go all in. Besides, her dad would hate knowing she was going to church, and somehow that made it a little more enticing.

She couldn't leave Jude hanging. When she told him he needed to show up early to church and actually talk to people, he agreed. If she would agree to go with him.

Her stomach had fluttered at the suggestion. Of course he wasn't asking her out on a date. People didn't go on dates to church, did they? No, he was just nervous and wanted someone to go with him.

She could understand that. How many times had she sat at home because she didn't want to go somewhere alone? Especially when Clay was out of town or just didn't want to go do something fun.

If someone was going to ask her to go somewhere with them, she was going to go. Even if it was church.

"Good evening," Jude's voice greeted her.

"Hey." She turned to meet him. "Good evening. It's a nice day, even if it's freezing."

"This is nothing," Jude said. "Wait until your first ice storm."

Felicity shivered. "I don't know if I can handle it. I wasn't born for cold weather."

Jude laughed. "No one was. But you adapt."

"Let's adapt by going inside," she said.

Jude nodded and jerked his head to indicate the way. "After you."

Felicity led the way up the steps with Jude behind her. The outside of the building was lovely, if a little older looking. Two large wooden doors at the top of the stairs opened up, and they walked into a small foyer.

"Welcome," a man and woman greeted her. "If you're as cold as we think, there's coffee in the welcome area through there."

Felicity smiled and nodded, following the way they pointed. When she saw Jan at the counter handing out coffee, it felt like she was really going to like this place.

"Felicity!" Jan called out when she saw her. "I'm so glad you're here."

"Thanks, I'm happy to be here too. And look, I dragged Jude along."

Jude looked completely uncomfortable as he lifted a hand in a wave.

"Great to have you both," Jan said, holding out two cups of coffee. "Felicity, this is my husband, Pete."

"Nice to meet you," the man said.

"You too," Felicity said.

"Oh, here's someone you should meet," Jan said. "Addison," she called out.

A woman standing a couple of feet away holding a small baby turned and came close. "Hey, Jan."

"Addison, this is Felicity. She's new in town, or visiting for now."

"Hi, it's nice to meet you. Sorry, I would shake hands, but I don't want to wake her up."

Felicity smiled and glanced at the sleeping baby on her shoulder. "Don't apologize. She's beautiful."

"This is Margaret Louise. She's six months old." She turned and tapped a man on the shoulder, and when he turned she said, "This is my husband, Ty."

"Hi," he said, reaching out to shake hands with Felicity. "Ty Riggs. Nice to meet you." Then he reached for Jude's hand. "Dr. Palmer, good to see you."

Jude seemed to be easing up as he reached out and shook hands.

"We go to a Sunday School class before the service. If you want to come with us on Sunday, we would love to have you," Addison said.

"Thanks, I'll think about it," Felicity said.

"We'd better get seats for the service," Jude said.

"It was nice to meet you," Addison said. "I know what it's like to be new in town. Let's get together sometime and talk."

Once again, Felicity was taken aback by the friendliness of people in town. She didn't even bother to say she didn't know how long she would be staying. "Thanks, I would like that." She waved as she turned and walked toward the sanctuary with Jude.

Inside the traditional sanctuary, the church felt familiar with the greenery draped along the walls and red bows on the pews. Most of her church experience included Christmas, so she wouldn't expect anything different. A few people sat in the cushioned pews, but most gathered in small groups around the room, talking, catching up. This must be what a small town really felt like. People who knew each other and kept up with what's going on in their lives.

A few people greeted Jude, and he nodded politely. They made their way to a pew near the back and took a seat. "Everyone knows you," Felicity said.

Jude took a deep breath. "It feels that way. I feel bad because I don't know most of them. Maybe a few, if they've been patients. But I'm not good at making small talk, so I don't have many conversations around town."

Felicity nudged him. "That's why we're here. It's time to make friends."

"Are we friends?" Jude asked abruptly.

"Of course," Felicity said. "You're the first person I met in town."

Felicity sat down next to Jude and took in the room. The air smelled of pine needles, and candles in the window flickered. It reminded her of a church they attended once when she was a little girl—wooden pews with hymnals in the back pockets. She settled in and took a deep breath.

How could a place she'd never been feel like home? It wasn't because she grew up in church every Sunday. Maybe it was because it reminded her of her childhood, back when her parents believed in going to church at least of couple times a year. Of course, back then she also believed in Santa Claus. Without meaning to, she let out a deep sigh. Maybe all of this was nothing more than a fairy tale. This vacation was a world where she didn't belong. And maybe this church was too.

"Are you all right?"

Jude's question startled her. She was so deep in thought, she'd almost forgotten he was there. And he was the reason she'd come. Part of her resolution was to help other people, and she was helping him get more involved in the town. Maybe church wasn't for her, but it could be for Jude.

She gave him a wide smile. "Yes, of course. Just taking in the room. It's beautiful isn't it? All decorated for Christmas."

Jude seemed to notice the decorations for the first time. "Oh, yeah, it's nice. A bit much maybe. But I'm not the person to ask about celebrating holidays."

"You don't have big plans for Christmas?"

"No. I don't make plans. I work most holidays. I don't have family here, and I don't travel. I work so people who want to can be off."

Felicity stared at him, unblinking. "Every holiday? Every Christmas?"

Jude shrugged. "Yeah."

"No." Felicity shook her head. "Uh-uh, you can't live like this. That's it. It's time for you to make friends and get to know this town. I'm officially taking over as your holiday planner. This year, I'm going to experience Christmas in Freedom because it's my only opportunity, and you're going to experience it because you've lived here for years and you never have."

Jude squirmed in his seat. "Oh, I don't know."

Felicity threw her hands up. "Well, I do. No excuses. We're doing this. I won't take no for an answer. As long as I'm here, if you're not working, we're experiencing the holiday here. Please say yes." She reached out her hand as if they were striking a deal.

Jude looked uncertain but reached out and took her hand to shake it. "Yes."

———

Jude could still feel the touch of Felicity's hand in his as they shook on their deal. He just couldn't say no to her. He had to admit, he didn't care that much about the town's festivities, but spending time with Felicity intrigued him. Why did she want to spend time with him? He was sure he had let her know how boring he was. Not talking to people, working on holidays, not even knowing the events that took place in town.

The question he had to ask himself was, was he happy living this way? If he was honest, he had to say no. He tried for a long time to convince himself he was happy. He was steady and safe. That was true. But that wasn't the same thing as being happy.

What was it people said, if you want something to change you have to do something different? If he wanted something to change, this was his opportunity. Felicity wanted a fun holiday season here, and she was asking him to be part of it.

Yes.

He would say yes. Yes to the Christmas activities and the festivals. Yes to Christmas.

And yes to Felicity.

9

Felicity couldn't believe Jude had said yes to this. Sure, she hadn't given him much option, but when she heard the school was hosting a Christmas dance as a fundraiser, she told him she was signing them up.

He hadn't even blinked. "Yes," he'd said quickly. She was pretty sure she heard him swallow and put his hand over his chest as if he needed to hold back his nerves. But he said yes, and she wasn't going to ask if he was sure.

Now she twirled in the small floor space in her hotel room. The silver dress ruffled at the bottom and swished with her movement. She had been sure she had nothing to wear to the event, but Addison had offered to loan her the dress she wore last year.

Felicity had never had a sister or even a friend to borrow clothes from. It was such a kind gift from the woman she barely knew, but she was learning that was normal for this town.

Her phone rang, and she glanced to see her father's number on the screen. She had sent a text to let them know she was safe, but she wasn't ready to talk. And she definitely wasn't ready for him to tell her to come home. She let it ring as she gathered her things.

When a ding indicated he had left a voicemail, she reluctantly picked up the phone and pressed play.

"Felicity, you will not continue to ignore my calls. I'm glad that you're safe, and I'm sorry that you felt we were pressuring you into this marriage. But you need to come home so we can talk about it. I know where you are. I've seen the charges on the credit card. But if you won't answer, I won't continue to pay for your trip. If I don't hear from you by midnight, expect that your card will be canceled."

Felicity gasped and her hand flew to her mouth. She should have known the happy feeling she'd had all day was too good to last. She dropped the phone on the bed and collapsed onto it.

Just then a knock sounded at the door. She blinked away the tears filling her eyes and went to open it.

"Hey," she said, trying to sound upbeat.

Jude stood in the hallway. He wore a smart suit and a red tie. She never could have imagined that he owned a red tie. Knowing he did made her heart flip-flop in a funny way, despite how upset she was.

His eyebrows furrowed. "What's wrong?"

"Nothing," she said, forcing a smile.

"I can tell. What is it? Your wrist? Head pain? Are you sick?"

Felicity couldn't help but let out a small laugh. Of course, he would think the problem was physical. If only it was. "No, no, nothing like that. I just had a call from my father, that's all."

"Oh," Jude said.

He wouldn't have a diagnosis for that.

"He wants me to go home."

Jude nodded thoughtfully. "Are you going to?"

"I don't know. I don't want to. But he knows where I am, and said he'll cut off my credit card so I can't pay for the resort."

"Oh," Jude said again, finding no other words to say.

"But I have so many plans and things I want to do here. I want to stay for Christmas. But even working at Wick and Sarcasm won't cover the cost of the resort. There's money in my bank account, but I don't need to spend too much on a vacation right now. I guess I should have looked for a less-expensive place to stay."

Jude's eyebrows rose. "I have a place," he said.

Felicity's eyes grew wide, her heart pounding at the thought. "Jude, I can't stay with you."

"No, I mean, not with me. I have another place. A cabin."

"You have a cabin?"

"Yes. My house and the cabin were both rental properties. My grandmother owned them as a side business. She left them to me when she died to help pay off my loans from medical school. I live in my house, so I don't rent it. But I have a cabin that I rent out. It's vacant right now."

"At Christmas? In the snow? How is it not rented out?"

Jude shrugged. "I wondered too, but maybe it's because it needed to be open for you."

Felicity laughed, but then frowned. "But I don't think I can afford that either."

"You don't have to pay me. It's empty anyway. Letting you stay won't cost me anything."

"Are you sure? There's power and a cleaning fee I'm sure. I can pay for that at least."

Jude held up his hand. "Felicity, I want you to stay." He paused and let the words hang in the air.

Felicity's breath caught, and she stood unmoving. Did he really mean that? He wanted to spend more time with her?

He cleared his throat, as if he couldn't believe he was saying it either. "We've made a plan for the holidays, and you're making me have fun at Christmas for the first time in a long time. I don't want you to go. So if letting you stay at the cabin helps, then I'm happy to do it."

Felicity swallowed and allowed herself to take a few slow breaths. He was having a good time. "So I'm fun to be around?"

He laughed then, and it broke the tension in the air. "More fun than me."

Felicity smiled. "I wouldn't say that. You haven't known me very long."

"Come on." Jude held out an arm for her to loop her hand through. "Let's walk to the dance, and you can tell me more about you. But even if you tell me you're not fun, I won't believe it."

Felicity felt lighter as they made their way down to the banquet hall where the dance was being held. As they walked in and saw the room, Felicity thought that the resort must donate the space to the school for the event. Surely, it was more expensive than a small local public school could afford for a fundraiser. Christmas lights lit up the room, round tables were decorated with green and red tablecloths with sparkling snowflake ornaments as the centerpieces. Long tables in the middle were brimming with hors d'oeuvres and dessert. Felicity almost licked her lips at the sight of a chocolate fountain surrounded by fruits, breads, marshmallows, and pretzels for dipping.

Dozens of couples mingled around the room, all of them in suits and dresses in all colors. Felicity looked over to see Addison coming toward them.

"Hey!" Addison greeted her with a wave. "That dress looks amazing on you."

"Thank you. It was so sweet of you to loan it to me. How lucky that we're the same size."

"I was happy to help." Addison gave her new friend a quick hug.

"You should keep it," Ty, Addison's husband said, coming up behind her. "She buys one every year for Christmas and then never wears it again."

Addison playfully elbowed him. "Maybe you should take me on more fancy dates so I can get more use out of them."

Ty laughed. "Once a year is enough." He straightened his tie. "Although I don't mind dressing up. It's better than my uniform."

"Uniform?" Felicity asked.

"Oh, yes, Ty is a police officer. I forgot to mention it.

I'm used to him being in uniform all the time. Seeing him in public in a suit is a treat. Last year he had to work during the dance, so he came in uniform."

"At least it's easy to get dressed for work," Ty said. "I guess it's the same for you, Jude."

Jude blinked a few times, as if registering the question. "Oh, yes, well…sometimes I wear a shirt and tie, if we have a meeting or something, but everyday wear is scrubs. I guess I didn't choose the job for fashion."

Felicity laughed. "That's good. Honestly, having to pick out dress clothes for work is one of my biggest stressors. If I could wear scrubs every day, I certainly would."

"I'm sure you look nicer than I do in scrubs," Jude said, stepping close to her.

Felicity felt her cheeks flush pink and looked to Addison and Ty, who were smiling and cutting eyes at each other over the compliment.

"We're going to get some food," Addison said. "Best to eat and have plenty of time for dancing." She grabbed Ty's hand and led him off.

Jude cleared his throat. "Do you want to eat?"

"Sure," Felicity said. "Do you plan to dance with me tonight?"

Jude blinked rapidly and looked at the floor. "Yes."

Felicity smiled. "Good. Because if you said no, I would have to argue with you."

Jude didn't want to argue with Felicity at all. Still it was a challenge for him to put more than two words together. How could someone so beautiful, fun, and interesting want to be with him? No, this was all temporary and just for her vacation purposes. In two weeks, she would be headed home and he would be here in Freedom. Would he slip back into solitude on the mountain when she wasn't there to drag him along?

There was no time to think about that now, since she was moving toward the food table. He carefully placed vegetables, grilled chicken kabobs, and salad on his own plate. He watched Felicity move to the dessert table and pick out a few items.

She looked over at him and frowned. "Is that all you're getting? Don't you want some chocolate or cake or something?"

He cleared his throat. "I don't do a lot of sweets." He'd seen enough strokes and heart attacks to know that he needed to keep his health in mind when he ate, especially this time of year.

"Oh come on, it's Christmas. You have to try dessert."

He looked up at her and bit his tongue to stop the "no" from coming out of his mouth. It wasn't as if he never had dessert; he just did it sparingly and wanted to make sure it was worth it if he was going to indulge. "All right. You pick," he said.

"I think some fruit dipped in the chocolate fountain is your best bet."

He nodded in agreement and picked up a toothpick. He stacked it with strawberries and banana slices before he ran it under the flowing liquid chocolate.

"There you go," Felicity said. "Now, let's go find somewhere to sit close to the front. I want to hear the live band when they start."

Jude felt a little relieved. Normally, he would feel self-conscious sitting up front anywhere. But if they were listening to the music, he wouldn't feel the pressure of filling the silence with conversation. He wanted to talk to Felicity, but the sooner she listened to him talk, the sooner she was going to find out how uninteresting he was. At this point, he wanted to keep her around as long as possible.

They made their way to a table, and Jude watched as Felicity enjoyed her food and swayed along to the Christmas songs the band was playing. Everything about her was effortless as she jumped into life.

A man Jude recognized as the school principal from his picture on "Principal of the Year" posters he'd seen around town stepped up to the microphone. "Hello, everyone. Thank you for coming out to support us tonight. We're thrilled that you're here because your ticket sales and the proceeds from the silent auction help us make improvements to our facilities and give students in Freedom the opportunity to participate in a number of programs they wouldn't otherwise be able to. But we really just want you to have a good time tonight. Please enjoy the food, and check out the items on the tables in the back. And now that the band is all warmed up, we hope to see all of you out on the dance floor." He lifted his hand in a wave. "Have a great night."

Felicity wiped her hands on her napkin and placed it on the table. "I think that's our cue." She pointed as several couples headed to the dance floor.

Jude stood and tugged on his suit jacket. "I'm ready if you are," he said, sounding braver than he felt. He held out his hand, and Felicity placed hers in it. Tingles rushed up his arm. He might have thought he needed to be checked out in the ER from the rate of his heartbeat, but he resisted the urge to place two fingers to his neck to count.

Felicity smiled as if she didn't have a care in the world as she confidently walked to the dance floor. The band played an upbeat version of "Joy to the World" as she turned and lifted her hand to Jude's shoulder.

He swallowed as he stepped close and put a hand to the small of her back. He should have had more water; his throat felt like it might close up.

"So what's it really like to work in an ER?" Felicity asked him. "I mean, it's not all brides in car accidents, I'm guessing."

Jude smiled. "No, so far in my career, you're the only one of those."

"Good. I like to be special."

"You are special," Jude blurted out before he could stop himself.

Felicity flushed pink and blinked her eyes rapidly. It was adorably beautiful. "I've never thought that. But it's nice to hear."

He wanted to ask her why she would say that. Of course, she was special. She had convinced him to come out of hiding and take a chance at life, simply because of who she was. She was certainly special to him. If only he knew how to tell her that. Instead he focused on her question. "No shift is the same. Sometimes, we never stop, and sometimes, it's slow. Although you never ever say that it's slow in the ER. That's just asking for a catastrophe. But some shifts I might see a lot of people with coughs and a couple of kids who need stitches. Other nights, I might deal with more major accidents. And then there's a mixture of all of it. So you could come see me work a shift one night and have no idea what my shift looked like the day before."

"At least it's not boring," Felicity said.

Jude tilted his head. "I've never thought that. I guess I think of myself as a boring person because I just go to work every day, but it's not boring there."

"No way," Felicity practically shouted as she gave him a disbelieving look. "I work in an office where I just stare at a computer. Now that's boring." She bit her lip as if she were rethinking what she'd said. "I mean, I did work in an office. Honestly, I'm not sure if I'll go back to work there. Or if my dad will let me."

Jude's heart squeezed in sympathy. "I'm sure he will forgive you in time. But is it what you really want to do? Work in an office, I mean?"

Felicity shrugged. "I don't know. I've never thought much about what I wanted to do. My parents paid for me to go to college and get a degree in business, and then I went to work in the accounting department. It's what was always expected of me, so I guess I didn't spend much time thinking of any other options."

Jude nodded slowly. "I decided very early in life that I wanted to be a doctor, so I didn't think about much else either." He paused and waited until she looked him in the eye. He wondered if he should continue. "But that was my choice. No one should choose for you what you want to do with your entire life."

Felicity pressed her lips together and pulled slightly away from him. "I know you're right. I guess I was too scared to try anything for myself. And maybe too much of a pushover to argue with my parents."

"I don't think you're a pushover, but maybe you were pushed over because you felt they had the power. Now you're here. You can choose what you want your future to be." Jude shrugged. "Maybe you want to go back and be an accountant at your dad's business. Or maybe you want to start a new career. Maybe you want to work in a candle shop in a small town. But whatever it is, now is your chance to decide. If you want to get out from under their power, this is the time."

Felicity took a deep breath and blew it out. "I think this is the perfect place for me to think and decide about all of that." She sighed. "But enough serious talk. This is supposed to be fun. What did you do for fun as a kid?"

Jude stared at her blankly for a moment. "You don't want to hear about that."

"You just told me that I get to decide what I want. What I want is to hear about you and what you did for fun as a kid."

Jude sighed. "Fine, but you asked for it. I did science experiments."

Felicity's eyes grew wide and she pressed her lips together as if she were trying not to laugh. Finally, she could hold it no more, and it burst out of her.

The sound sent joy through Jude's soul.

"I'm sorry, I didn't mean to laugh. I was just surprised.

What kind of experiments? Were you dissecting animals in your backyard?"

Jude grinned. "Not exactly. Although I did dissect a frog once. My mom almost died."

Felicity threw her head back and laughed. "That's amazing. I wouldn't have known where to start."

"Before that it was more like mixing baking soda and peroxide, and using test strips to determine if foods were acids or bases, that kind of thing."

Felicity wrinkled her nose. "I think we did that in science class once. I was never great at science. I did okay with biology where it was something you could look at and touch. But I almost failed chemistry in high school."

"If I had known you then, I could have helped. That's the other thing I did for fun, tutor people in math and science."

Felicity brushed a hair out of her face with her index finger. "You would have had your work cut out for you then. Not in math. I was good at math. That's how I ended up in accounting. Although what I do at work really isn't math, it's spreadsheets."

"You would probably be good at running your own business," Jude said.

Felicity furrowed her eyebrows as if considering this. "Maybe I would. But I don't know what kind of business it would be."

"Let's talk about something you might know that you want then," Jude said. "What do you want for Christmas?"

A smile played at her lips, and it was the most beautiful thing he'd seen all night. "I haven't known the answer to that for long, but I'm sure it's the right answer. I don't need or want any physical gifts this year. I just want Christmas here with no rules and no pressure. Just enjoying the season and being happy."

"Funny," Jude said, holding her hand a little tighter in his, "that's exactly what I want too."

10

Felicity tucked a blanket up under her feet as she settled in on the couch. Jude's cabin was a dream, even if it was cold, since the heat hadn't been turned on until about an hour ago. After the dance, Jude had walked her back to her room where she packed up all of her things and checked out, making sure the charge cleared the card before she tucked it away, planning not to use it again.

Jude had driven her to the cabin and helped her get settled as he showed her around. He was a perfect gentleman and left as soon as he got a fire going and made sure she had everything she needed. He promised to pick her up in the morning for coffee and breakfast before they went shopping for items for their gingerbread creation.

Felicity glanced around at the cabin. The two bedrooms led off the living room with a shared bathroom in the middle, and a kitchen ran the length of the house on the other side. It was a perfect cozy place for a small family or a couple to enjoy a getaway together. It had a woodsy decor, with a few touches of Christmas here and there. Jude must have someone who came out to decorate. She couldn't imagine him setting up Christmas trees and candles.

He did care about details though. He had made sure to point out where extra pillows were and everything from the thermostat to the lights for the back porch. But surely he didn't come out here for every guest. No, he seemed to be taking special care with her.

He had been doing that since the first day she met him. She was sure now that he didn't give his number out to every patient, and the way he took the box from her that day at the candle shop made her feel warm and fuzzy all over. Tonight had been easy and fun with him offering her his arm and opening doors for her.

Already she felt more cared for than she had growing up with her parents or with Clay. Sure, they had made sure she had what she needed and paid for everything in her life, but with Jude, he looked at her in a way that said he was truly concerned about her well-being. Maybe that was because he was a doctor and it was his job to make sure people were okay, but somehow, it felt like it was more than that.

She hoped it was more than that.

The thought surprised her. Why was she enjoying the attention of this man she'd only known for a few days? She had just gotten out of a relationship where she didn't take time to stop and think if it was really what she wanted. She had been pushed into spending time with him, and everything moved so fast.

No, she wasn't falling for Jude. That was just silly.

But was she forcing him to spend time with her? After all, she'd convinced him to say yes to all the events he'd never wanted to do before. What if she was the one pressuring him to do something he didn't want to do?

A sickening feeling came over her. What if she was acting just like her parents? Acting as if she knew what was best for him? She shivered, even near the warmth of the fire.

No, she wouldn't do this. Tomorrow she would offer him a way out. Jude was a grown man who was perfectly capable of spending his life the way he wanted. And if he wanted to live alone on the mountain, she would let him.

Even if she felt like a piece of her would go with him.

***

"Are you sure we have enough marshmallows?" Felicity asked.

Jude looked over at her and grinned. It was adorable, but she had asked this question about every item on the list. "I'm sure," he said. "But you're the accountant. Didn't you do the math?"

Felicity blew a strand of hair out of her face. "I'm an accountant, not an architect." She narrowed her eyes. "Do you think there are any architects in the competition? Maybe we should be worried about them."

Jude shook his head. "I don't think so. Architects are probably busy designing actual buildings, not important things like gingerbread towns."

"Right," Felicity said. "Maybe we should have done the

hospital instead. That would be something neat, to have a gingerbread hospital designed by a doctor."

Jude scrunched his face. "Nah, that would probably be boring. The hospital is a rectangular building with no interesting lines or design. It's functional, but not pretty."

"Yes, but it's important and helpful. Sometimes, helpful is more important than beautiful."

Jude wanted to say that he thought she was helpful and beautiful, but the words stuck in his mind instead of coming out. "So, you want to put the sidewalk here, right? What were we making that out of?"

Felicity pointed. "The white chocolate bars."

He nodded and began to unwrap the candy. "I'll start on that. You start putting together the buildings."

"Already on it."

Jude looked to see that she already had graham crackers built into boxes representing three stores. "Wow. You have a lot of practice building houses out of crackers and candy?"

She giggled. "Something like that. My grandmother would let us come to her house at Christmas and make gingerbread houses every year. When I was a teenager, she still wanted to continue the tradition, but we upped our game and started making famous landmarks."

"Wow, that's impressive. Would she have wanted you to come this year?"

Felicity shook her head. "No, she passed away three years ago. This is the first time I've done it since her last Christmas."

"Oh." Jude swallowed. "I'm sorry."

"It's all right," Felicity said. "You lost your grand-mother too. Were you very close?"

"Sort of." He cleared his throat. "My brother would say I was the favorite grandchild."

Felicity chuckled. "Sibling rivalry must be fun. I wouldn't know." She held a hand up in the air. "Only child."

Jude raised his eyebrows and tilted his head. "It's something all right."

"Where does your brother live now?"

Jude turned his attention to attaching the signs of the stores that Felicity had written with icing. "Brad still lives where we grew up: just down the street from my parents."

"Do you see him much?"

Jude cleared his throat. "No."

"No?" Felicity repeated, surprise in her voice.

Jude looked up and met her eyes. What would she say if he told her the truth? He didn't like to think about it himself. "We don't speak. Haven't in years."

Felicity's mouth fell open into an "O" shape. "I'm sorry. I didn't mean to bring up something painful."

Jude sighed. "It's all right." It didn't hurt as much to say as he thought it would. "It's just a fact. It's difficult, but I guess I'm used to it by now. "

Felicity bit her lip as if she didn't know if she should ask, but she finally did. "Did something happen?"

"You could say that," Jude said. "You know I said I tutored when I was younger?"

"Yeah."

"Well, the truth is I tutored people who were older than me. School wasn't just a hobby, it was my whole life.

I don't know, it just came easy to me, and I liked it. My brother was older than me, but they had me take some tests and skip ahead two years, then we were in the same grade."

"Oooo, that must have been great for you, but maybe not so much for him."

Jude nodded. "Yep. Not great is putting it mildly. He really hated it, and hated me."

"I'm sure he didn't hate you. But I can see how that would be hard for your relationship."

Jude took a deep breath and blew it out. "It got worse. School came easily for me, but not for Brad. So when it came time for our final exam, he…well…" Jude's voice trailed off, not wanting to even say it out loud.

"He wanted to cheat?" Felicity asked.

He nodded slowly. "When I wouldn't do it, well, let's just say things got worse between us. I went away to college and we haven't spoken since."

Felicity stood frozen with two bags of candy in her hands. "Jude, that's awful. I'm so sorry."

Jude met her eyes again. "Thanks. I guess I try not to think about it too much."

"I don't have any siblings, so I've never missed them, but I always wondered what it would be like to have one. I can't imagine having one but not really having them."

Without warning, Felicity dropped what she was holding and made her way over to him. She wrapped her arms around his neck. "I'm sorry."

The pain he had carried seemed to lessen at that moment. With Felicity near, he felt like maybe he could finally let go and enjoy life. "Thank you," he said, clearing his throat as she released him and moved back to her side of the table.

"Now," she said, "do you think we could build Christmas trees out of pretzels?"

Jude laughed and reached for the icing bag as he nodded.

An hour later, they were nearly finished. Jude would never have come up with this on his own. He might be smart, but Felicity had a creativity that he didn't possess.

Felicity smiled as she brushed her hands off. Jude noticed she had a smear of white frosting beside her left eye. "The judges will start making the rounds soon, and people will come by to see the displays. Let's clean up all the trash and wash up, then we can walk around."

Jude followed her lead, and they worked together in companionable silence. When the display was all ready, they left the table and made their way around the lobby to see the other entries.

They walked side by side, and Jude itched to reach out and take her hand in his. He had never had that urge before, but after the time they had been spending together, it felt natural. Still, he kept his hands to himself.

Felicity cleared her throat. "Jude, I need to tell you something."

His heart pounded at what she might have to say. "What is it?"

She laced her own hands together in front of her as they walked. "I just wanted to tell you that I appreciate you doing the gingerbread house with me, and it's been nice spending time together. But if you don't really want to do all the other Christmas things, you don't have to."

It might have been more comfortable if she stuck a knife in his side. Had she really just wanted him to help with the competition, and now she was done with him? Of course, she could celebrate Christmas on her own; only the competition had required a team of two. His stomach churned as he fumbled for a response, but all he said was, "Oh."

She stopped walking and grabbed his arm with both hands. "It's not that I don't want to. I just was thinking last night about how my parents talked me into things that I never wanted, and, well, look where that got me. I don't want to force you to celebrate all the Christmas events if that's just not who you are. It's okay if you don't want to."

Jude met her eyes and looked thoughtfully into them for several seconds. She was trying to do this for him. "What do you want to do?" he asked.

Felicity's gaze never wavered from his. "I want to do it all. I want to experience everything Freedom has to offer for Christmas."

He nodded. "And do you want to do it alone?"

"No," she said. "I want to do it with you."

He nodded. "Okay then." He continued on, but he noticed that she didn't let go of his arm. She loosened her grip, but looped her arm through his as they moved.

"Oh look," Felicity said, pointing at a table. "That one is Santa's workshop."

Jude followed where she pointed and smiled as he saw the elves made out of stacked candies and reindeer made of licorice on a bed of marshmallow snow. "That's clever."

They fell into a comfortable rhythm walking through the booths. They stopped to buy hot chocolate and peppermint candies to munch as they waited for the judges' announcement, which would be another hour away.

"You know," Jude said as they took a seat at a table for two, "I didn't know how fun these kinds of things could be."

"See," Felicity said, patting his arm, "I told you."

"I know, and you were right. Thank you for talking me into this. If it keeps going like this, it just might be my favorite Christmas ever."

Felicity smiled as she leaned close. "It's no contest for me. I already know it is."

11

Felicity tugged her coat around her as she climbed out of Jude's car. "Do you ever get used to it being this cold" she asked.

Jude shrugged. "I guess so. It doesn't bother me that much. I just try to wear layers if I have to be outside for more than a few minutes."

"Brrr." Felicity rubbed her hands together as they walked across the parking lot. "I'm sure glad they decided to do Christmas Caroling inside. I don't think I would last very long if we were walking house to house in a neighborhood. Even though that would be fun."

"I'm sure the people in the nursing home will appreciate the visitors. Some of them don't have family around."

"Addison said she and Nicole are bringing the kids, that always makes older people happy."

They moved briskly to the front door of Freedom Falls Senior Living Home. Inside Pastor Stephenson waited with several people who had already arrived.

"Good evening," he said, "I'm so glad you came." He reached out to shake their hands. "Jude, it's nice to see you."

Jude gave a curt nod, and his smile was tight. "Happy to be here."

Felicity watched as other people greeted him, some calling him Dr. Palmer, but a few of the guys from the party had started calling him Jude. That felt like a big shift. Maybe if he could just be Jude more often, then he could relax and enjoy hanging out with people.

"Hey Felicity," Nicole called out.

Felicity smiled as she made her way to her new friends. Nicole grasped the hands of two little girls, and Carson had his hands full with a baby. "Hi there," Felicity said.

"This is Julia, she's four, and that's Christine, she's two, and Carson has baby Johnny," Nicole said. She blew out a big breath of air. "I was excited to come with the kids tonight, but if we manage to keep them all together and no one cries it will be a Christmas miracle."

"Agreed," Addison said, popping a pacifier into baby Margaret's mouth.

"I'm an extra set of hands if you need help," Felicity said. She'd never held a baby as little as Margaret, but she could help entertain a four-year-old.

"I'll probably take you up on that," Nicole said.

"Everyone, let me have your attention for a moment," Pastor Stephenson said.

Felicity glanced at Jude who had been in conversation with Ty. It was nice to see him talking to someone and easing up a bit.

"We want to be respectful of the staff and residents while we're here. They have given us some time to walk through the halls and visit in the rooms of residents who are not able to leave their rooms. We'll split up into a few groups, so it's not overwhelming. We'll ask if we can sing them a song, talk with them for a few minutes, and move on. At seven o'clock we will meet together in the recreation room where a group has gathered and we will sing some songs for them. Please remember that they are just people and they love for you to visit and talk with them. You don't have to say anything particular, just ask them how they are, and see where it goes from there. Any questions?"

"Where's the bathroom?" little Julia asked loudly, causing the adults to chuckle.

Nicole's cheeks were red as she took the girl's hand and led her down the hallway.

Felicity smiled as she watched them go. As Pastor Stephenson spoke again. "I'll take a group, Nicole and Carson, Addison and Ty, and Jude and Felicity can come with me. Shayla will take another group. Jared and Alexis, and Aiden and Joanna, and Jan and Pete can go with her. The rest of you will be the third group."

Turning in the direction everyone started walking, Felicity stayed close to Jude. "I forgot to ask, do you sing?"

He laughed. "Not very well."

"Me either," said Felicity, "but I try and blend in with the group. And I do like music. Just don't give me a solo."

"Oh you didn't want that? I just told Pastor Stephenson that you would lead the group."

For a second her anxiety shot up, then she stared at

him as she playfully punched his arm. "You're joking. I didn't know you were capable."

"Oh, really?" he said, teasing in his tone. "Maybe you don't know me that well yet."

"So you're a big jokester, huh?"

"Actually no, not really, but I have my moments."

He didn't say anymore as they stopped in a doorway. The pastor asked if they could sing a song, Felicity couldn't see the person in the room since she was in the back, but they must have said yes, because the pastor turned and said, "Joy to the World," and off they went.

Felicity sang along, but only to the first verse. She wasn't familiar with any of the words past that. After that they sang "We Wish You a Merry Christmas", and then the pastor went in to speak for a moment. After that they moved a few doors down and started over.

Felicity smiled and waved as they passed more residents in their rooms until they made their way to the recreation room.

Her mouth fell slightly open at the number of people seated in the room. They filled the room from wall to wall. Some sat in chairs with walkers in front of them, and others were in wheel-chairs. Some seemed able to get around on their own. She couldn't help wondering about their stories. Did they have family who put them here because they couldn't care for them? Or because they didn't want to? Or were they here because they just didn't want to live alone?

The last one gripped Felicity's heart. Would she end up alone in her old age? Or even now? If her parents wouldn't speak to her again when she told them she was walking away from their path for her life, would she be alone?

Her chest ached and her throat closed up with emotion. She tried to paste on a smile as they gathered in a line to sing. When little Julia stood close to her and reached out for her hand, Felicity thought her heart might burst. How was it everyone in this town knew how to make her feel welcome and cared for?

The pastor called out songs for them to sing, they even took a few requests from the residents. The time was flying by and Felicity found herself able to focus on the music and the people listening instead of her own problems. Maybe that was what she came here to do - help others. She'd never done much community service, and maybe it was time she make up for it.

When the songs ended, the group spread out, talking to residents. Felicity wasn't sure what she would say to strangers but decided she needed to try.

To her surprise, Jude had no problem with this part.

"Hello there," he said, "I'm D..." he stopped himself, "I'm Jude, what's your name," he asked a woman who sat in a wheelchair and propped her chin on her fist.

"I'm Mary Wheeler."

"It's nice to meet you, Mary. Did you grow up around here?"

"Oh, yes, I lived in Freedom from the time I was six years old." With that she was off telling him stories of climbing the hill behind their house after the first snow, and walking to school when the elementary school was one building.

Felicity watched Jude's face as he listened. Maybe it

was his training from the emergency room where he met new people every day, but his face and tone of voice was genuine as he asked questions and listened intently to the answers.

When Mary needed to be taken back to her room to rest, Jude moved on to a man sitting in the corner alone. Felicity was sure the man wouldn't want to talk, but in only a few minutes, he was explaining to Jude what he did in the army when he was eighteen years old.

The hour flew by, and as the last residents left the room, waving goodbye and telling them Merry Christmas, Jude stood beside her. "Are you ready to go? he asked.

She stared at him in shock. "You were wonderful," she heard her own voice sounding breathless as she spoke.

He stepped back and his face turned an adorable shade of pink. "Me? No, that was nothing."

She reached out and put her hand on his arm. "Jude, you really connected with them. I had no clue what to say, but you made them feel special."

He looked at her in complete surprise. "I never thought about it that way. I guess I'm used to asking questions to patients. You just have to make it about them. If you ask questions, usually people start talking."

As they walked toward the door, Felicity thought about questions she could ask Jude. Because the more time they spent together, the more she wanted to know about this man.

12

Felicity pressed the doorbell then wiped her palms on her coat as she stepped back and pasted on a smile. Jude stood behind her, looking even more nervous than she felt. She couldn't remember the last time she'd been to a Christmas party at someone's house. The parties she attended with her parents were usually at the office or an event center or a country club. This would be nothing like that.

Addison opened the door carrying a baby on her hip. "Hey!" she shouted over the noise that billowed out of the house. "Come on in."

Felicity stepped inside and immediately felt the warmth of the room, not just the temperature. Christmas music played in the background, and the house smelled of bread and chocolate and peppermint. The house wasn't overly large, and people stood in every corner, but everyone was talking and laughing like it was the best place to be.

"Oh, I love your ugly sweater," Addison said to Felicity.

"Thanks," Felicity said, proudly running her hands over the tacky red-and-green wool with jingle bells attached all over it. "Look at what we found for Jude."

Jude tried to make an angry face to match his sweater.

"Oh the Grinch!" Addison squealed. "I love it!"

Addison looped her arm through Felicity's as if they were old friends and led her into the kitchen. "Jude, the guys are down in the basement looking at Ty's pool table he just bought at a garage sale," she said, turning her head to look over her shoulder. "Go on down and make yourself at home."

Felicity's heart registered a tiny bit of panic at being separated from him. That was silly, since they weren't a couple. He had only agreed to spend time with her because she'd challenged him to. He could go hang out with the guys; that would be good for him. That was part of the point, right? For him to get to know people in his own town. Still, she was getting used to him being around, and being separated from him when she was already nervous around people she didn't know made her want to go somewhere else, just the two of them.

There wasn't time to think about that since Addison started introducing Felicity to everyone. Felicity smiled as she was introduced to Nicole, Gretchen, Jess, and Haven.

"So you've all known each other for a while? Did you all grow up here?" Felicity asked.

Addison shook her head. "Not me. I grew up in Georgia and moved here nine years ago." She waved a hand in the air. "But that's a long story. Nicole and I have been close for a long time."

"So you grew up here?" she asked Nicole.

"No, not me either. I'm from North Carolina. But Jess grew up here."

Jess nodded. "That's right, and Haven too. Ever since Mom moved back, my whole family is here."

"And my husband, Chris, is from here," Gretchen said. "I'm a transplant from Vermont, but I'm here to stay. And I doubt the kids will move away, or at least I hope not."

"I can understand," Felicity said. "I haven't been here long, but it seems like the kind of place that gets in your blood. It will be hard to leave."

"So why not stay?" Addison suggested.

"Oh, I don't think I could do that." Even as she said it, Felicity wondered why not? If she didn't work for her dad anymore, she could move. Would she really move away from where she grew up? Nicole, Addison, and Gretchen seemed happy to have moved here. Maybe a change was exactly what she was looking for.

She let her mind hang out there for a minute while the other women discussed gifts for their kids for Christmas. She caught a snippet here and there—a bike, a doll, something about a dinosaur. Gretchen asked, "Did anyone sign up for the Secret Santa event?" and that sent the conversation into a flurry of who was participating in the town gift swap and who wasn't and what a fun idea it was.

"So." Nicole sidled up next to her. "Tell us about you and Jude. I couldn't believe it when Addison said he was coming tonight. He hardly even says hello at church."

"He wants to get more involved in town. I think he was just nervous, maybe a little shy, and he needed someone to help him jump in and meet people."

Addison flashed a playful grin. "And that someone was you?"

Felicity felt her cheeks grow warm, and it wasn't from the coffee Addison had pressed into her hands. She shrugged. "I wanted to enjoy Christmas in town, and it seemed like a good idea for us to go to events together."

"And now?" Nicole asked, wiggling her eyebrows. "You're spending a lot of time together. Is there something going on between you?"

"Oh no," Felicity said quickly. Maybe too quickly. It seemed like the right thing to say, since she'd just run away from her own wedding and didn't know what she was doing with her life. "We're not a couple. We're friends. Just hanging out at Christmas so we don't have to go alone."

"That's too bad," Nicole said. "If someone managed to get the quiet doctor to come out of his shell, they really shouldn't waste it by just being friends for Christmas."

Jude stood outside the kitchen and hung his head. The guys were all about to come upstairs. He had just been the first one up, just in time to hear Felicity tell the woman that they weren't a couple.

She was right, so why did her words hurt so much? His stomach twisted in pain to hear her say they were just friends. Did he really want to be more? He hadn't said that. She hadn't either, so maybe he was just reading into it. His thoughts were drowned out by the sound of the men entering the room, laughing as they talked about how badly Ty had missed the last shot in the game of pool with Duncan.

"It was truly a spectacular failure," Duncan said.

"Yeah, yeah," Ty said. "Let's get some dessert, and I'll renew my strength before our rematch."

"No way," Jeremiah spoke up. "I called winner, and after that Jude can play. Right, Jude?"

"Um, oh, yeah, sure," he said, trying to focus.

"Come on," Ty said, patting Jude on the shoulder. "Addison's been baking for days. Let's get some food."

Jude hung back and wandered slowly into the kitchen behind the crowd. He told himself to stand to the side and let Felicity talk with whoever she wanted to. Only a moment later, she was at his side.

"Hey," she said, as if they had been apart for longer than a few short minutes.

"Hey," he repeated, searching for something else to say. "Did you meet everyone?" he asked. Even as he said it he wished he had come up with something better.

"All the girls, yes," Felicity said.

Addison made her way over and finished the introduction of the guys, pointing out who went with whom. "That's Duncan, he's Jess's husband and Ty's partner on the police force. Jeremiah is married to Haven, and he's also Jess' twin brother. And Carson is Nicole's husband."

"You probably don't remember, but we've met before," Carson said.

Felicity squinted her eyes as she looked at him, and recognition dawned on her face. "You were there at my accident. You're the EMT who got my suitcase out of my car."

Carson nodded. "That's right."

"Thank you so much. You were a lifesaver." She laughed. "Not only because you actually took me to the hospital, but I wouldn't have anything to wear if it weren't for you."

"Happy to help," he said. "How's your wrist?"

Felicity lifted her arm and showed her brace. "Not bad. Jude fixed me up with this. Really it doesn't hurt much now."

"You still need to be careful," Jude reminded her. "And you have to go to the orthopedic."

Felicity grinned at him and brushed her shoulder against his. "I will, I promise."

"That's right, follow doctor's orders," Addison called out. "But right now, we have house rules, and house rules say we need to eat some of this food. And make sure you get a ballot for the Ugly Christmas Sweater Contest. Ty, are we waiting for Toby and Jared to come back?"

Ty shook his head. "Toby texted and said he had some-thing to take care of and Jared took Alexis home. I guess she wasn't feeling well." He shrugged. "I'm sure I'll get more details later."

Addison frowned. "I hope she's all right. But if we're not waiting, then everyone, let's eat!"

Everyone milled around and chatted as they filled their plates.

Jude made his way to the living room, and Felicity followed with her plate full of sweets. At her insistence, he had put a cookie on his plate, and he carried a mug of hot apple cider.

In the living room, most of the seats were taken. A couple of the wives sat on their husband's knee as they nibbled their goodies.

Jude watched Felicity sit on the floor in front of the fireplace and thought once again how confident she was. He probably would have stood and leaned awkwardly against the wall until he could make an excuse to leave, but she just sat down in the middle of everything. He took a deep breath, trying not to think that people were watching him as he moved to sit beside her.

"Mm, Addison, the chocolate chip cookies are delicious," Felicity said around the bite in her mouth.

"Yes they are, until you try the macadamia nut, which is absolutely amazing," Haven said.

"Oh, you know what would be fun? Next year, we should have a cookie contest. Everyone can bake a couple dozen, and we'll do a taste test and vote," Addison said.

Nicole shook her head. "It might be fun, but we know who would win," Nicole said, laughing.

Jude got hung up on the words "next year." Would he be here next year? If Felicity wasn't here to drag him to parties, would he still go? Or would he even be invited? It surprised him that he felt sad to think about her not being here.

A whining noise from the next room drew his attention.

"Oh, that's the dog. Ty, you should let him out for a few minutes. He's going crazy hearing all these voices and knowing he isn't included."

Jude watched as Ty walked from the room and in just a moment a black lab came bounding into the room. He recoiled in anticipation of the dog jumping straight into his lap. He must have closed his eyes without realizing it. When he opened them, he was relieved to find no dog on top of him.

Beside him, Felicity was giggling as the dog licked her. "That's a good puppy," Felicity said, running her hands along its back.

"Sorry," Ty said. "He's big, but he does still think he's a puppy."

"What's his name?" Felicity asked.

"Partner," said Ty.

"He seems like a great dog," Jude said.

"He is. Addison and I met because of him." Ty smiled. "It's my favorite story."

The conversation turned, and Jude sat listening to the group of friends talk. He settled in and began to enjoy himself. He didn't need to be the center of attention, and he was happy to listen to others and join in their laughter.

Felicity sat contentedly next to him, patting Partner and talking.

Jude watched her and a thought came that surprised him. What if they really were a couple? If she stayed here, was there a possibility for them to be together? He pictured himself sitting next to her in their own home, maybe with a dog, enjoying the fireplace and some Christmas treats.

He glanced at Felicity and watched her laugh at a joke someone made. Yes, he could picture all of that. But would she want the same thing? Or was she really only here for the holiday then she would disappear from his life forever?

When she looked back at him and their eyes met, deep inside he desperately hoped for a chance to convince her to stay.

13

Felicity cupped her hand over a cinnamon sugar candle and inhaled deeply. "Mmm," she said. "I'm not going to make any money working here if I keep smelling these."

Ashley laughed. "I'm glad you like them. But don't go broke. I have a few sample sizes in the back you can have."

"Really?"

"Yep. Just tell everybody to come here for their Christmas gifts."

Felicity bit her lip. "I bought Christmas gifts for my parents before I left town. I wanted to get them something nice as a thank you for all they did for the wedding. Now I won't even see them at Christmas. Who knows if they even want to speak to me."

Ashley put a hand on her shoulder. "I'm sure they do. Families fight and get mad at each other, but in the end, they usually work things out. That's what love is."

Felicity nodded as she turned to stock more candles on the shelf. Had she really known what family was about? "My family is more like a business partnership. And the more I think about it, the more I realize I was an employee who was part of the image of the business. If I've damaged that image, then I might just get fired."

Ashley gave her a weak smile. "You can always stay here and work for me."

Felicity chuckled, feeling a little better at the thought. "Thanks. I might take you up on that. My dad would die if I became a shelf-stocker and cashier permanently and didn't put my accounting degree to good use."

Ashley's jaw dropped open. "You have an accounting degree?"

Felicity nodded. "Mmhmm. And I minored in business marketing."

"I had no idea. You don't need to be in here doing this. You need to help me make sense of my books. I love making candles, and owning the shop is a dream, but I'm a mess when it comes to actually running the business."

"Really? I would be happy to take a look. You know, I've been thinking, do you sell online?"

Ashley scrunched her face. "I tried once, but I only had a couple of sales. I have a website, but there's nothing on it. I'm just too busy to update it."

"Maybe I can look at that too. I think you could do a lot of business that way. And then maybe you could hire more full-time help."

"Like you?" Ashley winked.

"As much as I would love that, no, probably not me. I don't know what my next step is. But I really appreciate you having me here while I figure it out."

"I'm happy to have you for as long as you want to stay."

Ashley turned and went through the curtain to the back room.

Felicity turned the candles over in her hand, reading the names—Sideparts and Skinny Jeans, Currently Reading, Imaginary Boyfriend, Lavender London Fog. How had Ashley ever been so creative to think of these? And she was so brave to turn it into a business.

Her thoughts ran back to when Jude said she should start her own business. She had run the idea over in her mind a few times since then, but nothing came to mind. She wasn't creative like Ashley with her candles, and she couldn't bake like Jan, or run a resort. But hadn't all of them just relied on their own special skill set to get started?

What was special about her that she could use to start a business? As much as she hated to admit it, she was good at the job her dad had asked her to train for. She had liked math when she was a kid, but there had to be a more creative way to use it than staring at spreadsheets.

She sighed. Maybe something would come to her if she kept thinking about it. Of course, there was still the possibility all of this would just be a short trip in the land of make-believe and she would return to her normal life working at her father's company.

Her phone dinged then, and she went to the counter to check the message. A text message from Jude read:

There's a Christmas party tonight at work. I think they didn't tell me ahead of time because they thought I wouldn't come. It's very low-key and I'll still be working, but I'd love it if you want to stop by.

Her heart fluttered at the invitation. Yes, they had

agreed to attend Christmas events together, but being invited to a work Christmas party felt like more than that.

It felt like a relationship.

Was Jude starting to think of her that way? Were they becoming more than just two people who had a Christmas agreement? No, no, that couldn't be. He was just someone who needed a little push to get into the holiday spirit, and she was just someone who didn't want to be alone at Christmas.

Surely, he felt the party was a part of their agreement. That was all there was to it.

Before she could think about it anymore, she typed out a quick reply. *Sure, sounds fun!*

Still, she couldn't stop thinking of the words he had sent. "I would love it."

Would Felicity love it if they became more than Christmas companions?

JUDE TRIED TO FOCUS ON HIS PATIENTS ALL AFTERNOON. His co-workers were getting their jobs done, but the excitement of the Christmas party hung in the air. At first, he couldn't understand why this would be such a highlight. Was a work party really such a great part of the holiday? But the more he thought about it, the more he realized these people thought of each other as friends—family even. After all, they spent more time with each other than they did with other friends, or probably even family. Why wouldn't they want to celebrate together?

He would have to make more of an effort to talk to

people at work. For too many years he had come to work with his head down and set about the task of taking care of people. Was that the right thing to do when he was ignoring the people he saw every day?

"You ready for the party, Dr. Palmer?" Nurse Sandra asked. Her face said she expected him to scowl and say no.

"Yes, I am. Sounds like it's going to be a good one."

Sandra stepped back, clutching her tablet to her chest, clearly stunned.

Jude smiled as he strode down the hall to see a patient. This could be the new Dr. Palmer. Someone who didn't grumble about gatherings, and someone who said hello and smiled at people. Felicity would like that.

He stopped dead in his tracks in the middle of the hall-way. Felicity. He hadn't admitted it to himself yet, but he cared what she thought. He couldn't stand for her to know him as a grumpy doctor who didn't talk to anyone for weeks. He wanted to be better.

He wanted to be better for her.

His heart was stirring within him at the thought. What would it be like for them to be something real? Not just people going to Christmas events together, but people who did everything together?

Because if he told the truth, he wanted to do every-thing with Felicity.

Jude cleared his throat as he walked into the exam room and listened intently to the patient's concerns, which was most important right now, but when he walked out of the room and down the hall for the Christmas party, he couldn't wait to see the woman who was quickly becoming an important part of his life.

Almost an hour later, Jude stood in the corner sipping some tasty Christmas fruit punch. The nurses and doctors meandered in and out of the break room. Some were here just for the party, but those who were on the clock came back and forth from working and taking care of patients. Thankfully, it wasn't too busy tonight, although Jude knew better than to say that out loud.

He heard a voice at the door say, "I think he's in here." Looking up, he saw a nurse pointing the way into the break room, and then he was rewarded with the sight he'd been waiting on.

Felicity looked beautiful as always. He didn't think he had seen the deep-blue sweater she wore with jeans and a pair of brown boots. She came close and smiled. "Hi."

"Hey." Before he could stop himself he opened his arms and wrapped her in a hug. He breathed in deeply. "Mmm, you smell like cinnamon."

Felicity pulled back, and he noticed a tinge of pink on her cheeks. "It's the candle shop. I tend to smell like whatever Ashley is making."

"Well the cinnamon one is good."

"It's Cozy Christmas Cabin. I think it's my favorite."

"I think you're my favorite." Jude's eyes grew wide as the words tumbled out of his mouth without permission.

Felicity paused as her eyes met his. She didn't say anything for a moment, but then she smiled and her eyes twinkled more than the Christmas lights that hung from the ceiling. "I think you're my favorite too," she said.

Jude breathed out, feeling as if his heart might burst if she had said anything else. "Want some Christmas punch?" he asked. "I think they're about to start some sort of gift game, but I didn't bring anything, so we can just watch."

"Sounds good," Felicity said.

Jude fixed her a glass, and they made their way around the best they could in the crowded room to find a seat. "If I get a call, of course I have to go out. But please wait and I'll come back to you."

Felicity smiled. "Where else would I go?"

Jude's insides warmed all over at her smile. "Just prepare yourself. It might get loud."

Felicity wrinkled her brow. "Because of an emergency?"

He jerked his head toward the staff members forming a circle in the middle of the room. "No, because of this."

At that moment, one of the women shouted above the crowd, and the game began.

Jude and Felicity watched and laughed as people opened gifts, sometimes in excitement and sometimes to the tune of laughter at a gag gift.

After a nurse opened a package containing a large pair of Charlie Brown Christmas socks, the room erupted in laughter. Felicity leaned close and spoke loudly near Jude's ear. "Why didn't you bring a gift?"

"I didn't know about the party."

"Do they usually not tell you?"

He cleared his throat and dropped his gaze to the floor. "No, they do. But I complained last year."

Felicity gave him a disapproving look. "Why would you complain about a Christmas party?"

He shrugged. "I guess I thought we should focus on our work. But I see now that everyone is still doing their job. They're just having fun while they do it. Maybe that's what I've been missing out on for a long time. I've been doing my job and living my life, but not having fun doing it."

Felicity nodded as if she understood. "I think I've been doing the same thing. I'm sorry that it took a big disappointment and an accident to figure that out." She hooked her arm through his. "But I'm not sorry that I was here when I did figure it out."

Jude stared into her eyes as she spoke. He leaned close, and his gaze flicked down to her lips. If he leaned in, would anyone else even notice? He didn't care if they did, and just then it was as if there was no one else in the room. He looked back to her eyes as if asking for permission. She didn't look away, and he moved forward.

"Dr. Palmer," the voice boomed over the speaker overhead. "Dr. Palmer, you're needed in exam 4. Dr. Palmer to Exam 4 please."

Felicity let out a little giggle as she leaned back and released his arm. "Go on, go save a life. I'll be here waiting when you get back."

14

Felicity woke the next morning with a smile on her face. The Christmas party had been wonderful. Actually, she hadn't paid much attention to the party. It was loud and she didn't know anyone except Jude. But the time with him was wonderful, even if it was interrupted every few minutes.

The only thing that would have made it better was if he got to walk her out. Maybe then they would have been able to get that kiss that she thought he wanted to give her.

Her stomach fluttered at the thought.

If only she didn't have to wait five more hours to see him. He said after working late in the ER he usually slept in to catch up. Felicity was sure he must have been tired. He still had hours to go last night when she left the party.

It didn't matter anyway; she had to be at work at nine. He promised to stop by and bring her lunch.

At home, when she woke up at five in the morning, she felt rushed to get everything done in time to leave for work and drive through traffic. Here, everything was different. She was awake at seven and felt like she had all the time in the world. It only took about ten minutes to get to Wick and Sarcasm, and there wouldn't be any traffic.

Felicity yawned as she sat up in bed and stretched her arms over her head. After a quick shower and a breakfast of eggs and toast, she sat on the couch and wondered what to do with herself for the next hour.

She stood and went to the bookshelf to inspect her choices. Someone besides Jude must have stocked these books. Most were romance stories. There were a few Marcus Warner books—she'd heard of that author but never read the books.

Something caught her eye: a navy-blue hardcover that looked a little old. She ran her fingers over the gold leathering. "Daily Devotions for a Peaceful Walk with God." She tilted her head and finally decided to take it to the couch. She'd never read much of the Bible on her own, and she wasn't sure how to start. But maybe she could handle a devotion book.

Sitting on the couch, she wrapped herself in a blanket and opened to the first page. The introduction explained that each day had a verse and a few thoughts and ended with a prayer. That seemed simple enough. She turned the page.

Day 1: Perfect Peace

Come to me all of you who are weary and burdened, and I will give you rest. - Matthew 11:28

We make life complicated. Taking on burdens, stress

because of work, bills, broken relationships and the heaviness of life.

The world can feel painful and challenging and we don't know where to turn when we are disappointed or struggling through difficult circumstances.

That's not the life God created us for. Jesus said in John 10:10, "I came that they may have life and have it abundantly."

What does that mean? When we have life in Jesus, it's not a list of rules for doing all the right things. Jesus came to die for us so that we could be free. Free from sin and death, and free to live life in perfect peace with God.

When you give your life to Jesus, He forgives your sins so you can have a relationship with God, but he doesn't stop there. He sends the Holy Spirit to dwell in you, giving you access to the Father through prayer and relationship. He doesn't just want to keep you from eternal punishment for sin, He wants you to walk with Him all the days of your life.

This doesn't mean everything will be perfect, in life we will still have troubles, but we won't go through them alone. Jesus is always with us to lead and guide us and to comfort us.

Without Jesus, our lives will always be missing something. We can never fill the hole in our heart that God created to be filled only with Himself. When we surrender to Christ and ask Him to be Lord of our life, He fills us with His love, His joy, and His peace, and we are satisfied in Him.

John 14:27: Peace I leave with you; my peace I give to

you. Not as the world gives do I give to you. Let not your hearts be troubled, neither let them be afraid.

Dear Heavenly Father, Thank You for loving me and rescuing me. Thank You for making a way of peace and allowing me to walk with You. Quiet my heart and mind and teach me to focus on You every day. I trust You with my life and know you have good planned for me. Amen.

Tears filled Felicity's eyes and made it too difficult to read the page any longer. How long had she been looking for peace and joy? Her parents had chosen money and success, and while she went along with it, she knew there had to be something more. But even here she had been looking for happiness in celebrating a holiday and going to all the events she could. What if this book was right? What if she could never be satisfied with this life?

At that moment, the tears spilled down her cheeks as she realized she knew it was true. Nothing here could satisfy her. What was it the pastor had said on Sunday? *"Jesus came to give us life, and without Him we will never know true joy."*

She wiped at her eyes and didn't waste another minute. "God," she began, "I don't really know how to do this. I'm not like other people who grew up in church and know the right words to say. But maybe that's not what's important. God, all I know is, I want the peace and joy that the Bible talks about. I want to have Jesus in my life. I don't know what I'm doing with my life now. Maybe that's a good thing. God, I believe Jesus came to earth to save me, and I believe that if You cared enough about me to send Your Son, that You must have a purpose for me.

So I give You my life. Fill me with your love and peace and show me how to live for You."

Felicity opened her eyes and put her hands to her chest. It felt as if a weight lifted from her, and she felt lighter than she ever had. This was what had been missing in her life. Jesus. "Thank You, God. I don't know what's next, but I'm ready for it. Whatever You have planned for me."

She wiped the tears—happy ones now—that drifted down her cheeks. She hadn't known that one simple prayer could change her life in a moment.

Felicity couldn't stop talking to God all morning. She prayed silently to Him as she went to work and as she went through the motions of her job. She smiled at everyone who came in and wanted to tell every person that today her life had changed.

Ashley asked her why she was humming.

"Am I?" Felicity asked in surprise.

"Yes, you've been doing it all day." Ashley poked her elbow into Felicity's ribs. "Is it Jude? You two sure have been spending a lot of time together. I still can't believe it. I've never seen him say more than two words to anyone."

Felicity felt her cheeks flush. "He's really nice. We have been….getting to know each other. But that's not why I'm so happy today. It's part of it, but not all of it."

She wanted to say more, to tell Ashley the whole story, but she was distracted by the sound of the bell and looked at the door. She prepared her customer smile, but when she saw Jude, her smile got even bigger. "Hey!" she shouted, moving from behind the counter and rushing to him. She ignored the bags of food he was carrying and threw her arms around his neck.

"Oof," Jude said as they collided. "Hey, I'm happy to see you too."

Felicity pulled back and put her hands on his arms. "I have something to tell you. Come on." She turned to yell over her shoulder. "Ashley, I'm on lunch break." Normally, she would have made sure to ask permission, but she was too excited. She led Jude through the back and up the stairs to the space above the store. An old couch and coffee table sat in the middle of the room, and Felicity rushed to sit down and waited for Jude to join her.

Jude carefully set the food on the table and looked at Felicity. Written in his eyes were a mixture of confusion, concern, and excitement. "What is it?"

Felicity took a deep breath, and pressed her palms together in front of her to contain her energy. "This morning, I found a Bible devotional book on the shelf at the cabin. I opened it and started reading and it was just like it was talking to me. I've been searching for something my whole life, and I didn't even know it, but it was God. He's always been there waiting for me. Today, I prayed, like really prayed on my own, for the first time in my life. I'm a Christian now, Jude. I'm a follower of Jesus."

Jude's mouth fell slightly open. "Wow, Felicity, that's wonderful." He leaned forward and wrapped her in a hug.

"Isn't it?" she gushed. "I've never felt so happy. I just feel like whatever happens now, I know that God let me go through everything in my life to lead me here. He could have saved me anywhere He wanted, but I will never forget that He saved me in Freedom."

She couldn't read Jude's expression. His smile was tight, and he cocked his head to the side.

"What's wrong?" she asked.

"Nothing." He gave her another quick hug. "This is wonderful news. I, just, um…" His voice dropped off.

"What?" Felicity pressed him as she put a hand to his arm and held his gaze.

He shrugged. "I'm so happy for you. I guess I just don't understand exactly how you feel. I've heard people say that before. But I've been in church my whole life. I know who Jesus is, and I've read the Bible before." He sighed. "But I work in a hospital where I see a lot of the evil, sadness, illness, and hurt of the world. I know God put me there to help, but sometimes it's hard to have peace and joy and see the things I do."

Felicity's heart felt as if it might break inside her chest. She didn't know what else to do, so she wrapped her arms around him and didn't let go. "Jude," she whispered, "God doesn't want you to carry that burden. You're right that He put you there to help, but Jesus is here to help you. He wants to give you rest. If you haven't experienced that, maybe you haven't really experienced Jesus."

Jude leaned back to look her in the eyes. "What do you mean? I told you, I've been in church my whole life. My parents taught me to pray and read the Bible when I was five. I give money to support the church, and I only miss Sunday if I have to work."

Felicity nodded. "All of those are good things, but it's not the same as knowing Jesus personally. I thought that too. I thought my whole life if I was a good person and worked hard to be successful and maybe volunteered for a charity then I would be good. But I've never had peace in my life until today. You don't have to decide right now, but think about it. I'll pray that you can really know Jesus, because now that I do, I understand the difference, and it's the most amazing thing I've ever experienced."

Jude set his clipboard down on the desk and leaned back in his chair. Felicity's words had stuck with him all day, all evening. And now that it was dark and he knew that work would get busier as it always did, he wanted to put it out of his mind. He couldn't be worried about something like this while people needed him here. Besides, didn't the fact that he was here, giving his whole life to take care of other people, say enough about his character?

He went to church on Sundays. He even gave to the church. No, he hadn't made a lot of effort to be involved and get to know people, but that was changing now, wasn't it? What did Felicity think he needed to do? Join a committee or go on a mission trip? His mission was right here at the hospital.

Still, her words were like a pounding heartbeat in his mind. *"You haven't experienced Jesus."*

Taking his glasses off, he set them on his desk and rubbed his eyes. What did that mean anyway? He knew about Jesus. He'd heard all the Bible stories and could quote verses he learned as a kid. He shook his head. No, he didn't need to worry about this. His religion was just fine, and he was doing his part to help out in the world.

"Dr. Palmer, we have an accident victim coming in," the nurse said. "Ten minutes out."

Jude stood and returned his glasses to their proper place. "I'll be ready." He wouldn't wait to hear them come in. He would be at the door when they arrived. His heart picked up the pace as he moved through the hallway. Car accidents always did that to him. He knew they would become more frequent, with the snow and ice they would deal with through the winter.

He tapped his fingers on the doorpost as he watched out the door and saw the ambulance pull in.

An elderly woman was pulled out and wheeled toward the emergency entrance.

"Female, seventy-four, hit on the passenger side by a truck that ran a red light."

Ran a red light? Jude clenched his fist at his side as he ran alongside the gurney. People were so careless and selfish.

"I'll be all right." The woman's voice was frail.

A worn, brown leather object caught his eye. The woman clung to it on top of her chest. There were blood droplets dripping down the side.

"Ma'am, could I take this for you, so we can clean it up?" Jude asked. He hated to see an item that precious be ruined or stained.

"Oh no, no, I'll hold onto it, unless it's interfering. I've had this Bible since I was a little girl."

Jude's chest felt like an explosion inside. "Bible?" The word tumbled out of his mouth as if it couldn't stay inside.

"Yes, I never go anywhere without it. Jesus saved me sixty years ago, and I've walked with Him ever since."

Jude pressed his hand to his forehead. No, he couldn't do this. He was the one who was always calm and collected in the ER. He didn't get emotionally involved. That's what made him good at his job. He could focus on caring for the patient. But with Felicity's words echoing in his mind, and now this woman's Bible staring him in the face, how could he keep his focus on her care?

He shook his head and squeezed his eyes shut. He needed help. What could he do? Before he could realize what he was doing, his heart whispered a prayer. *God, help me focus, help me do my job and help this woman. I need Your help.*

When he opened his eyes, calm washed over him. He reached for the woman's hand and gave it a squeeze. "Ma'am—"

"Violet," she interrupted him.

"Violet, we're going to take good care of you."

With that, he clicked into motion. He checked her heart, her blood pressure, and asked her where the worst pain was. He wasn't surprised when she said her head, since he could already see the laceration on the side that would require several stitches. He couldn't explain it—he always felt confident in himself at work—but this felt like he didn't even have to think. It was as if his speech and his motions were directed before he could think about what he was doing next. Violet had a number of small injuries, but it was the smoothest examination he could ever remember doing.

"Violet," he said when he had finished checking her over, "I'm going to send you for a CT scan, just to make sure that everything is all right. I'm sorry to say that you're also going to need some stitches on your head and on this cut on your arm."

"Don't apologize, son. At my age, I'm used to getting bumps and scrapes, and I'm just happy the good Lord has allowed me to make it this long. He must have something important for me to do here today."

Jude tilted his head. "That's a nice way to look at it."

"Oh, honey, it's the only way to look at it. If I thought my life was just a random collection of events with no purpose, I would just melt down and cry. But I know the Lord has ordered my days. That old car had seen better days, and I'm sad for it to go, but God wanted me here today for a reason."

Jude couldn't take his eyes off her. He didn't even have to wonder. God had sent her there to meet him. He all but collapsed onto the stool beside her bed. He sighed, giving in to what he knew was coming. "Violet, you really know Jesus don't you?"

Violet smiled as she patted his hand. "Yes, I do. He's walked with me through everything in my life. Through friendships, and marriage, and children, and loneliness after my children moved away, and sadness after my husband passed. Jesus has never left me, and I will go to my grave thanking Him, not just for saving me, but for being with me and guiding me my whole life."

Jude folded his hands in front of him. "What does that

mean, though? I go to church, and I do my best to help people. But I don't think of my life as 'walking with Jesus.'"

"Oh, son, then you're not living. You're just going through the motions. When you walk with Jesus, you talk to Him every day. You read the Bible and pray. When you ask Him to be the Lord of your life, He sends the Holy Spirit to live in you. That's what Jesus called 'life more abundant.' Trust me, life is much more abundant with Jesus."

Jude gave a weak smile. "Thank you, Violet." He stood. "I'll order those tests, and someone will be in to stitch you up."

"Can't you do it? I would enjoy talking with you more." Her eyes were kind as she looked at him.

He cleared his throat, needing to get out of the room. "I'm sorry. I have to check on other patients. But someone will be in soon."

He stepped out from behind the curtain and walked down the hall. He was headed toward the office, but his feet kept going past the door. Air, that's what he needed. Even if it was cold, he needed to be outside of the building for a minute to gather his thoughts. He fought to keep from sprinting out the back door. Once outside, he took deep breaths as he wrapped his arms around himself. His lab coat wasn't enough to warm him in these temperatures, but it was better than inside where it was suffocating.

He wished he could shake it off, walk back inside and go on with his shift, but it was no use. As he stared up at the stars, one thought consumed him: He had never truly walked with Jesus.

After a few gasping breaths trying to push the thought away, he surrendered to it. "God," he said out loud, glad that no one else was around to hear him, "I don't know what You want from me. But I know You're trying to get my attention. I thought Felicity was just here to help me open up to the town, have some fun, and learn how to have a life." He took another deep breath. "But if what Violet says is true, I can't have a true abundant life without You." Another thought hit him like a ton of bricks, and he wrapped his arms tighter around himself. "I've been afraid that if I let You in, that if I gave You my life, that I would lose. I didn't want to give up control or be taken advantage of. I see now how dumb that was. You can't take advantage of me. You've already given me a gift that I can never repay."

He squeezed his eyes shut, and his body and soul flooded with warmth, despite the temperature. "God," he said, "I've believed in You, but I've never given You my life. I've never allowed You all the way in and asked You to be Lord. I want to walk with You. I want the life that Jesus came to give me. I want to follow You. Show me how. My life is Yours."

Jude opened his eyes and stared again at the sky. The stars seemed to shine brighter, and Jude felt as if a light inside him came on and shined as bright as the stars. "Okay, God," he whispered, "let's get back to it."

16

*J*ude couldn't wait to see Felicity again. Not only because he wanted to be around her as much as possible, but because he couldn't wait to share his news. He was too excited to sleep in the next day, and he drove to the cabin on autopilot because his brain was elsewhere, thinking of Felicity and how they would spend the next few days.

When Felicity opened the door, he opened his mouth to blurt something out, but snapped it closed again when he saw that she was on the phone.

She held up a hand and then motioned for him to come in. She shivered as he pulled the door shut behind him. The look on her face concerned him. She didn't look happy.

"I understand what you're saying, but I'm standing my ground," she said. She turned back to Jude and put her hand over the phone. "My mom," she mouthed.

Jude's eyes grew wide as he opened his mouth in a wide "O." This would probably take a while. He collapsed on the couch and tried not to eavesdrop on the conversation as Felicity moved into the bedroom. It was hard not to hear her side of the conversation.

"Mom, I love you, and I do hope we can work things out in the future. I'm sorry for what happened, but I'm not coming home for Christmas. After the holidays, when everyone has had time to process and calm down, we will talk about this. I need to go now. I promise I'll call in a couple of days. Bye, Mom."

Jude was impressed with how calm and mature she sounded. "Hey," he said, putting his arm around her shoulder as she fell onto the couch next to him.

She blew out a big breath. "Hey, sorry about that."

"Don't be sorry. That had to be a difficult conversation."

Felicity turned to face him. "You know, I thought it would be, and it wasn't easy, but I don't feel as emotionally wrecked as I thought I would."

"That's good."

"Right? She's upset about what happened, and she said they were expecting me for Christmas. When I told her no, she told me that Clay is going to be there so we can work things out."

"Oh," Jude said. "What did you say?"

Felicity shrugged. "The truth. There's nothing for me and Clay to work out. Me and my parents, on the other hand, have years of baggage to sort through. But I'm not doing that on Christmas. It's waited this long. It can wait a couple more days."

"I have some news that can't wait," Jude said, reaching for her hand. "And it's because of you."

Felicity bit her lip, dropped her gaze to their joined hands. "Okay," she said the word as if it were slightly painful. "What is it?"

"I thought about what you said." He chuckled. "Actually, I tried not to, but I couldn't help it. And then this woman came into the ER gripping her Bible as if it were the only thing that mattered in the world. She talked to me about Jesus, and I knew He was trying to get my attention. I understand what you were saying. It's not just about going to church and trying to do my best. Walking with Jesus is something completely different. I was afraid at first, but I gave my life to Jesus, and I'm not afraid anymore."

"Oh, Jude, that's wonderful." Felicity threw her arms around his neck and squeezed until he thought he might run out of air. She released him and cleared her throat as she scooted back on the couch. "I'm so glad for you. I hope you feel the same peace that I do."

He nodded. "It's amazing."

"That's why I can talk to my mom and stay calm. They've always made me think that being successful is the most important thing, and that meant that the business was the top priority. That's why they want me to come home. They need to save face by cleaning up the mess I made. But it's not the most important thing. I want to celebrate Christmas, not with expensive gifts and catered food, but in church with people who are thankful that Jesus came to earth."

Jude took her hand again and gave it a squeeze. "I feel the same way," he said. "That's what I wanted to talk about. We have just a couple of days before Christmas, and I want to make the most of it. What are your plans for the rest of your trip?"

FELICITY SNUGGLED BACK INTO THE WARMTH OF THE CAR'S heated seats and sipped the hot chocolate from her mug. "This is fun," she said.

Jude grinned from the driver's seat but carefully kept his eyes on the road. "Look at that house." He pointed.

"Oh this one is part of the competition," Felicity said, reaching for the paper to read. "It says there are twelve houses that entered the light show contest this year. When we're done with the tour, we can vote on the website for our favorite."

"I've never seen so many lights," Jude said.

Felicity giggled. "My parents would die if they saw a house like this." She reached for the volume on the car stereo to turn up the Christmas music. "My mom doesn't even decorate. She has a professional come do it. But it's all greenery and red and battery-powered candles in the windows. Nothing twinkling or plastic or gaudy." She took a long sip of her drink. "What about you? Did you decorate for Christmas growing up?"

"Yes, we had everything you just said you didn't." Jude laughed. "Twinkling, plastic, and probably a little gaudy."

Felicity reached for his hand. "I'm sure it was nice."

"It was. We had decorations that we used over and over again for years, so it was fun to pull them out and see them again in December. When we were kids, it would be a fun family night." His eyes darkened as he thought about the more recent years and sighed. "But by the time I was in high school, my brother usually had better things to do. I would help my mom get out the boxes and put everything up. It would take us a whole day."

Felicity bit her lip as if she didn't know what to say. "I'm sorry about your brother," she finally said. "Maybe one day the two of you can finally reconcile."

Jude shook his head, not wanting to think about it anymore. "Let's talk about these lights. Do you like this one the best?"

Felicity gave him a lopsided grin. "We haven't seen the others yet."

He smiled. "Yeah, but sometimes you see something and you just know it's your favorite. You don't need to see the others because that one already claimed a place in your heart."

elicity's heart flickered inside her like the glowing candles that lit the windows of the church. Her soul was quiet for the first time maybe ever, as she entered the sanctuary next to Jude. He reached for her hand, and when he laced his fingers through hers, she knew he felt the same way she did. Not only were they walking in to celebrate the birth of Jesus, they were walking in together, just the way she wanted it to be.

Neither of them spoke as they walked toward the front and found the closest seats they could. It was nothing like the first time they came to church together where they took seats a comfortable distance in the back. Felicity knew it didn't matter, but it felt like she could be more a part of it if she was closer. Truly, she just couldn't get enough of it. Being in church, reading the Bible, praying to God. This was what her soul had been missing, and now she wanted as much of it as she could possibly get.

She sat next to Jude and kept her hand in his. "This is nice," she said, her smile bright.

A child came into the row holding a box covered in red velvet. The girl was shy as she held out the box. Felicity smiled at her as she reached in and took a candle. "Thank you," she said.

The girl smiled back before hurrying off to people in the next row.

"I haven't been to a candlelight service in forever," Jude said. "At least ten years."

"I've never been to one," Felicity admitted. "We went to church a few times on Christmas Eve, but we never had candles."

"It's the best part," Jude said, squeezing her hand.

"I think all of it is the best," Felicity said. "All I've ever known about Christmas is bright lights and professional decorators and Santa Clause with expensive gifts. This is the real Christmas."

Jude nodded, and he turned in his seat and put his arm around her shoulder. "I'm glad I'm here with you," he said. They fell silent then as the pastor moved to the front and the piano music that had been playing softly quieted.

"Good evening, and Merry Christmas Eve," he said. "We're so glad you've joined us tonight as we celebrate the eve before the birth of Jesus Christ. Whether you are someone who has attended our church for many years, or whether you've joined us for the first time this evening, we're thrilled that you're here. You've heard it said that Jesus is the reason for the season, and we believe that. But it's more than just this season. It's our prayer tonight that you know and love Jesus every day of your life.

"Please stand with us and turn in your hymnals as we sing together to worship our Savior."

Felicity stood, and Jude reached for the hymnal in the pocket of the pew in front of them. He turned to the hymn and held it out for both of them to see.

They sung along to Christmas hymns that Felicity had heard hundreds of times on the radio or playing over a speaker in a store during the month of December, but she'd never listened to the words and sung them as if they had such a true meaning before. Singing of the night Jesus was born, how the angels came to announce the good news to the shepherds. Her eyes filled with tears thinking that the good news was for her too and that now she understood why Jesus came to earth. Jude reached over and squeezed her hand, and she knew he understood it too.

When they sang "Silent Night," the pastor lit his candle, then two men at the front lit their candle from his. The men walked down the aisle lighting the candle of the first person in the row, and then each person lit the candle of the person next to them.

Felicity watched as the room began to fill with candle-light. Her heart pounded as she lit her candle and shared the flame with Jude. She didn't stop the tears that fell down her cheeks as she sang along. It was all too beautiful. She didn't deserve Jesus, and she didn't deserve forgiveness. What if she wasn't here tonight? What if she hadn't run? Silently, she whispered a prayer of thanks that God had a plan for her and that even in the midst of pain, he had used her circumstances to lead her to Himself.

When the service ended, Felicity looked over and smiled at Jude. No words were said, but when their eyes met, an undeniable connection passed between them.

They had shared something special tonight, and it would be part of their lives forever.

"Felicity!" a voice squealed.

She looked up. "Addison." Before she finished the word, she was enveloped in a hug.

"I didn't know you were coming tonight."

"I wouldn't have missed it. It was a beautiful service."

Addison nodded. "Lighting the candles always makes me cry."

"It did me too. I can't imagine spending the night before Christmas anywhere else."

Jude and Felicity were greeted by a few other people. But Felicity's own words echoed in her heart. It was true. She couldn't imagine being anywhere else, and she didn't just mean church. She meant Freedom. Here, in this place that was new and strange only a couple of weeks ago, now felt like home more than anywhere she'd ever lived.

She kept quiet as she and Jude walked hand-in-hand to the car, her mind rolling over the idea, what if she stayed here? What if there was a future here for her?

And most importantly, would that future include him?

***

JUDE POKED THE FIRE IN THE CABIN AND CAREFULLY CLOSED the screen before he settled in on the couch. Felicity came from the kitchen and handed him a cup of hot cocoa, complete with so many marshmallows he didn't know how he could drink it. "Thanks." He smiled. She was just like those marshmallows, filling his life up to the brim.

She sat with her own mug and tucked her feet underneath her on the couch. "I was thinking about something."

Jude's heart pounded at double normal speed, trying to think of what she might say. With Felicity, it could be anything. She could go from zero to one hundred in a second, and now he knew he would let her pull him right along with her.

"What's that?" he asked.

"I need to go home."

His heart slammed against his ribs. "What?" he practically shouted before he could stop himself.

She held up a hand. "Calm down, let me explain."

What was there to explain? If she went home, that meant she was leaving. Would she really drop everything they had? "You want to go home?" He ran his hands through his hair, his brain rapid firing every possibility for the future. "I mean, I guess I knew you had to go sometime. But now?"

Felicity reached for his hand. "Listen. I need to go home to sort things out. I told my parents I would come home after Christmas so we could talk."

"And what will you say to them?" Would she apologize and go back to her job and life there?

She took a deep breath and blew it out. "I've been working on that. I don't know if my dad wants me to come back to work. And unless things have changed in the last few days, my mom is still trying to get me to come back and work things out with Clay."

Jude swallowed hard. "Does he want to work things out? Does he still want to marry you?"

Felicity looked into his eyes and shrugged. "I don't know. But I don't want to marry him, and nothing is going to make me change my mind."

"But do you want to still work for your dad?" Jude had never wanted someone to say no so desperately.

"Honestly, I don't know about that. He might make that decision for me, if he fires me. But if I go back, I don't think it will be forever. I love it here in Freedom. When I left my wedding that day, all I knew was I was running away as fast as I could. But all I could think about was that I was running away from something. I didn't have any idea that I could be running to something else. I didn't know I would find Freedom, and I definitely didn't know I would meet you."

Jude wiped a palm on his shirt before he reached to take her other hand in his. "Can I say something now?" he asked.

"Mmhmm." Felicity nodded.

"I had no plans to meet anyone. I was just going through the motions of life. My job was good and I was good at it, and I thought that was enough. Then you showed up. You pushed me to step out and do something that was just for fun, something new and different. And I was terrified. I almost backed out, but something told me I needed to keep saying yes. And, Felicity, I wanted to say yes to you." He blinked rapidly and cleared his throat. "I didn't know this was possible, but, Felicity, you have changed my life, and it's all because I'm falling for you."

She smiled and blinked away tears that were filling her eyes. "I'm falling for you too. I didn't even know what that felt like before. At first, I just thought it was nice to have someone to go to events with, but I had that with Clay. But he never made me feel this way. When you reach for my hand, I get butterflies every single time. I miss you every moment that I'm not with you."

Jude closed the distance between them, wrapping his arms around her. "Felicity," he whispered, "you're everything I never knew I needed, and so much more than I could ever want." He couldn't wait another second to press his lips to hers.

She kissed him back with all the passion that she put into everything she did. Jude drank her in as if he were a man who had lived in the dessert for years. And in so many ways, maybe he had. His hands moved up and down her back as he kissed her again and again, and she pressed herself closer to him.

Breathless, he pulled back to look her in the eyes. He reached to brush a tear from her cheek. "You're crying," he said, sounding more like a question than a statement.

She nodded. "Happy tears. I didn't know I had any of those. But it's all so overwhelming to feel this way. My life has changed so much since I came here, and it all started with you."

Jude kissed her once more. "It makes me happy to hear you say that. I feel like the one who is lucky to have met you, so if I have even one tiny part in making you happy, then I'm a happy man."

Felicity turned and snuggled into him as she pulled a blanket over her lap. She sighed a long, happy sigh. "I could sit here forever with you."

He kissed the side of her forehead as he wrapped his arms around her. "Then let's just enjoy tonight. I don't want to think about you leaving, even for a little while. So let's just pretend we can stay here forever."

18

Felicity sat in the same spot as the night before and stared out the window of the cabin at the snow. She truly could have sat there with Jude forever. But that had been cut short when he needed to leave. He couldn't stay late when he had to report to work early in the morning.

Now, Christmas morning, she sat alone. There were no presents, not even a Christmas tree in the house. And yet, it was the most wonderful Christmas morning of her life so far. If only Jude could be with her. She hoped to go by the hospital later today and surprise him, but she knew he might be busy. He said the holiday was always a busy day in the ER.

She wasn't sure what she would do with herself the rest of the day. Everyone was busy with their families.

She sighed. She really should call her parents and tell them Merry Christmas. Rising from the couch, she went to the bedroom and picked up her phone. She smiled to see a text from Jude. *Hope you have a wonderful Christmas morning.*

She stiffened as she saw another text.

Clay.

I've tried to call. I don't know what happened and I wish you would talk to me. Felicity, we can work this out. I still want you to be my wife. We can build a life together if you will just come back to me. Maybe I'm not the most romantic guy in the world, but I would be a good husband. If you'll come home I think I can show you that. I care about you, Felicity.

She sank into the couch, staring at the words. He was right; he probably would be a good husband. And she did believe he cared about her. A sigh escaped her lips. But now she knew there was more. More life than her parents had let her see, more choices than sitting in an office counting money for the rest of her life, or becoming a corporate wife, going to events where she had to put on a smile and talk to people she didn't know.

No, that life wasn't hers anymore.

But still, Clay deserved an explanation—and an apology. She squeezed her eyes shut as she prayed. "God, how do I do that? I don't love him, and I don't see myself having a future with him. But I don't want to hurt him."

She thought of her parents again too. Yes, they had run her life for a long time and pressured her into decisions that she didn't want to make. But she still cared about them.

At that moment, she knew what she had to do. Without another thought, she stood and pulled out her suitcase.

It was time to go home.

Jude sat down in his chair and tried to catch his breath. The morning had been non-stop. If it wasn't a burn from a Christmas candle, it was putting stitches in a guy's head after a collision with his new drone.

It was the same every year. Christmas gifts caused more accidents than anyone would ever imagine. Normally, it made him sad and depressed. This year he prayed for every patient he treated—that they would heal quickly, but also that they would see Jesus in this holiday and that would be more important than any other gift.

Thankfully, they hit a lull, and he thought he could grab a bite of lunch. Just as he stood to go to the break room, he looked up at the sound of someone coming down the hall. His eyes lit up and he broke into a full smile when he saw her.

"Surprise!" Felicity said.

He made his way around the desk to her as quickly as possible. Wrapping her in his arms, he placed a kiss as long as he dared to her lips. "Hi," he said.

"Hi, Merry Christmas."

"Merry Christmas," he repeated. The best Christmas ever. "How has your morning been?"

He thought he saw her eyes grow sad for just a second, but she smiled before he could be sure. "Good," she said. "Quiet, but not in a bad way. It was nice to sit and pray and enjoy the morning."

"Not too lonely?" he asked.

"I didn't mind it. Although I do wish you didn't have to work."

"I know, me too. Maybe next year I'll be off." He heard himself say it and quickly glanced at her to see what she thought.

She grinned at him. "Maybe."

"Have you eaten? I was just going to get my lunch from the fridge."

"Hmm," she said. "I have a better idea." She turned and went back into the hall and came back in with a picnic basket. "I brought you Christmas lunch."

Jude's mouth dropped open as he watched her carry the basket to his desk and start to pull things out.

"I've got turkey and dressing, sweet potatoes, salad, and an apple pie for dessert."

"Where in the world did you get all of this? Did you make it?"

Felicity blushed. "No, I wish I could. But Jan made the apple pie, and the food is from Evelyn's restaurant. I picked it up yesterday and just had to reheat it. Maybe one day I'll learn to cook."

"It looks good to me." He reached for her hands and kissed her. "This is the most wonderful Christmas lunch I've ever had. Thank you, sweetie."

"Sweetie?" she repeated, tilting her head at the name.

He searched her eyes. "Is that okay? I didn't plan it. It just came out. I won't do it again if you don't like it."

She stood on her tiptoes and kissed his cheek. "It's wonderful, just surprised me. No one has ever called me a nickname like that."

"Not even your parents?"

She laughed. "Oh no, definitely not. My dad calls me Felicity, and that's it. My mom calls me Felicity Patricia Rosemary Keaton if I'm in trouble."

"Wow, that's a lot of names."

Felicity rolled her eyes. "I know, right? They wanted to name me Felicity, but Patricia and Rosemary are both my grandmothers' names, and they wanted to use them both, so I got three names."

"They didn't want to save one in case they had another daughter?"

"Oh, no, I was definitely going to be the only one. My mom had a really rough pregnancy and swore she would never do that again. My dad wanted a son, but she wouldn't even try again, in case it was another girl."

Jude furrowed his eyebrows. "But they were glad to have a daughter, I'm sure."

Felicity shrugged. "I guess. You would think so. If I had been a son, I think my dad would have been grooming me to take over the company instead of working in the accounting department. I know, women can run companies, but my dad's pretty old school. That's why he was so happy when he met Clay. He was the son he never had, and he wanted nothing more than to learn to run the company."

Jude wrapped his arms around her. "I'm sure your dad loves you."

Felicity sniffed. "I know. But I think he will be happier with Clay. Even though we didn't get married, he can still have the son he wanted."

Felicity stood back and waved a hand in the air. "Let's not talk about that now. Let's just eat some food and celebrate Christmas together." She winked at him. "Babe."

A little while later, Felicity packed up the food and left. Jude promised to stop by the cabin when he got off that evening. Felicity had tried to tell him he could go home and sleep, since she knew he would be tired, but he wouldn't want to be anywhere but with her.

He changed out of his scrubs and into jeans and a sweatshirt before he left. Walking in the door to the cabin was like coming home, even though he didn't live there. The sight of Felicity in a house made it home to him.

"Hey, sweetie," he tried the nickname again.

She smiled. "I like that." She kissed him. "Are you exhausted?"

"Yes," he said, collapsing on the couch. "But I'm happy to be here."

"Do you want to watch a movie or something?"

"We could, but I would probably fall asleep," Jude said, covering a yawn with the back of his hand.

Felicity laughed. "I could poke you if you snore."

"Who said I snore?"

She shrugged. "Just a hunch."

"What are your plans for tomorrow?" he asked, changing the subject.

She bit her lip as she sat on the couch and his stomach flipped in worry. "I need to talk to you about that," she said.

He sat up, not tired anymore, only concerned. "What is it?"

She sighed. "I told you I need to go home, and it's time. I'm packed and I'm leaving for home in the morning."

Jude was glad he was already sitting because the way his head was spinning, he might have fallen over. His heart beat wildly at the thought of her leaving. "Are you sure? How long is the drive? Do you want me to go with you?" He didn't even know if that was possible, but he felt desperate to stay with her.

She reached out and put her hand on his arm. "It's going to be all right," she said. "But no, I need to do this on my own."

"But when will I see you again?"

Tears filled her eyes now. "I don't know. I don't know what the plan is. All I know is I need to go home. Jesus has changed my life, and I don't regret coming here at all. But it still hurt other people that I left, and I need to apologize and make things right with them. I want my parents to have what I have, and if there's any chance of that, they need to see that I've changed."

"But..." Jude took in a gasp of air. "Will you come back?"

"I've been praying a lot about that. I hope I can, but I don't know the future. I want to be here, I want to be with you, but I have to figure things out."

Jude nodded, even though he wanted to disagree with her. "I can't stand the thought of you leaving," he said. "But I don't want you to stay here and be unsettled. I wish you would let me come with you."

"I know, and I appreciate that more than you can know. But, Jude, there's something else I need to tell you."

Jude crossed his arms in front of his chest, hoping to protect himself from whatever news she had. What could be worse than her leaving?

"God has clearly impressed on me that I need to go home and talk to my parents. I've been praying for you too, and I think you need to go home and see your family."

Jude put his hands to his chest as if he'd been injured. "What? Why?"

Her voice was gentle, but he hated the words she was saying. "Because your relationship has been broken. And if there's any chance of repairing it, you have to be the one to reach out."

"Why should I? He was the one who was wrong. He hates me because I wouldn't help him cheat, and he thinks I ruined his life when he did that to himself. I didn't do anything wrong."

"I know that. That's what makes it hard. But what if he wishes he could change things but he thinks you'll never forgive him? What if he's met Jesus and he's different now?" She bit her lip. "Or what if he hasn't met Jesus and you can be the one to show him by offering forgiveness?"

Jude bristled against the idea. "I don't know." When he looked at her eyes, so earnest and full of hope for him, he relented. "I'll think about it."

She leaned over and kissed his cheek. "I'll pray about it."

"When do you leave?" he asked, feeling the pain in his gut.

"First thing in the morning."

"Can I see you then?"

She shook her head. "If you come over, I don't think I'll get in the car."

He grinned. "That's the idea."

She smiled at him. "Let's enjoy tonight, and then we'll say good-bye."

"Let's start that movie. Pick a nice long one, and you can poke me when I snore."

Felicity giggled and reached for the remote.

Two hours later, the credits rolled. Jude had barely managed to keep his eyes open, but now he was wide awake, knowing his time with her was ending.

Felicity stood and waited for him to join her. She slipped her arms around his waist. "You need to get some sleep," she said.

"I would rather stay with you," he said. "I don't want to say good-bye."

"It won't be forever."

"How do you know?" he asked. Even asking made him sick to his stomach.

Felicity had no answer, and he pulled her closer to himself. He reached for her chin and tilted her face up to kiss her. Slowly at first, and then more intensely as his lips moved with hers. It nearly broke him when he tasted the tears on her lips.

Finally, he pulled back and pressed his forehead to hers. Knowing he would never be ready to let go, he whispered the words, "Good-bye, Felicity." He kissed her one last time, then he let her go and turned and walked out the door.

As he climbed into his car and looked at the window, he hoped for one more glance of her. There was none, and he thought it was best. If he saw her, he might go back in and never leave. Fear gripped his heart. What if that was

his last glance of her? What if this had all been a temporary Christmas vacation and she went back to her life?

"Please, God," he prayed as he started the car. "Please bring her back to me."

19

*F*elicity stepped out of her car in the driveway and pressed her hands to her back as she stretched. She stared up at her house in the upscale neighborhood. Home. Was that really what this was? Her parents had bought the house for her last year when Clay made the engagement official. She had moved in and was supposed to be "setting up house" for them as Clay made plans to move in after the wedding. A terrible thought occurred to her. What if he was here? Surely, he wouldn't do that. But his apartment lease was up at the end of the month. Where would he go? She pressed her hand to her forehead, thinking about the mess she had left behind.

Opening the trunk, she pulled her suitcase out, remembering only a few weeks ago when she packed her bag for what she expected to be a very different trip. Her wedding dress was in the trunk, rolled up in a plastic bag from the hospital. Her mother would just die if she saw it.

She sighed as she closed the trunk and made her way inside. When she stepped through the door, the house didn't feel as cold as she had expected, and it didn't have that musty smell of a house that had been closed up for weeks. Her fear was confirmed when she heard the garage door open and turned to see Clay pulling into the driveway. She dropped her suitcase and walked into the kitchen where she sat on a stool and waited.

It was several minutes before Clay came in through the garage door. He must have needed a minute to collect his thoughts.

"Hey," she said when she saw him.

He stared at her for several moments in silence. "Hey," he finally said with a sarcastic bite to his tone. "You didn't even tell me you were coming home."

She sighed and crossed her arms in front of her. She didn't want to fight. "I'm sorry. I should have. I was going to call you when I got in. I just didn't expect you to be here."

"Why wouldn't I be? I live here. We're supposed to live here together, remember."

Felicity's mouth dropped slightly open. She did know, but she hadn't expected him to move in after what happened. "Oh, I, uh… I mean, I guess so. I just thought maybe you were still at your apartment. We can't both live here. We're not married."

He moved to where she was in the kitchen and stood just in front of her. "That's not my fault," he said.

"I know…" Her voice trailed off. Suddenly, she wasn't sure how this was going to help things.

"But I'm still willing to do that. We can go to the cour-thouse today. We don't have to have a big wedding if that's what you're afraid of. If you were nervous, you could have told me. Cold feet are perfectly normal."

Felicity gathered her resolve. "Clay, I didn't get cold feet." She stood to face him. "I came back to say that I'm sorry."

He gave a sigh of relief and smiled. "It's okay. We can move forward and put this behind us. Maybe one day we'll even laugh about it. I can forgive you."

Felicity shook her head, trying to think of how she could convince him. "No, Clay, you don't understand. I'm sorry that I hurt you. Really I am. I should have been honest a long time ago, but I thought maybe I could do it. We could get married and maybe we would be happy. We would have a normal life, married, working at my dad's company, and life would be fine. But that day, sitting there in my wedding dress, I was supposed to be the happiest woman in the world, but I wasn't. Clay, we're not right for each other. Yes, we look good on paper, but even you said you care about me. You didn't say you love me."

Clay shoved his hands onto his hips. "Of course, I love you. I care about you, and I'll take care of you. I'll work hard and give you everything you need."

"Clay." Felicity kept her voice gentle. "That's sweet, and I think you really mean it. But that's not all there is to life. Sure, marriage isn't all about sparks and fuzzy feelings, but have you ever once just missed being around me and wished you could just be with me and sit together as we talk about the future?"

"Felicity this is ridiculous. All we ever talked about was a future together."

"I know, but I've come to realize that's not the future I

want. It's what you want, and it's what my parents wanted for me, but it's not what I want." She reached out and put a hand on his arm. "Clay, I think there is a woman out there who does want that, and she will be a wonderful wife for you, and you will be the perfect husband for her. I think you'll even get butterflies when you're around her. But that woman isn't me."

Clay sighed as if defeated. "I don't know about that. But I'm not going to force you into a marriage you don't want."

Felicity gave him a kind smile. "Thank you, Clay. I came here to say I'm sorry, and to ask you to forgive me for hurting you."

He looked at her and tilted his head to the side. "Forgive you?"

"Yes. Even though I don't think I'm supposed to marry you, I shouldn't have let it go that far. I shouldn't have said yes to a commitment I couldn't keep. Will you forgive me for that?"

Clay shrugged as if he were uncomfortable. "Sure, I guess."

"Thank you," she said.

"But what do I do now?" He held his hands out in the air. "I moved in here. I guess I was hoping you would come back and see me living here and just decide to get married and stay. That was pretty stupid."

"It's all right." She bit her lip. "You moved everything out of your apartment then?"

"Yes. I turned over the keys."

"Well, I won't kick you out. I'll go stay at my parents' house until we can figure this all out." A terrible pit formed in her stomach. If only Clay would offer to stay with her parents. She was sure they liked him better than her.

"Thanks," he said. "That would be a big help."

Inwardly, she groaned. "I'll just gather some things and get out of your way." She wished she could tell him to leave, but it was bad enough that she had left him at the altar. She couldn't also make him homeless.

Within a few minutes, she had been to her bedroom and bathroom and pulled out clothes, personal items, and toiletries to last her a few days. She would have to come back, but this would do for now. She had hoped for a couple of hours to rest after the drive before she needed to face her parents, but maybe it was better to get it over with.

Back in the living room, she found Clay sitting on the couch with his head in his hands. She cleared her throat, and he sat up quickly. "I'm going now," she said. "I'll be back in a few days. Maybe by then we can have a plan."

He nodded. "I'll start looking for a place."

Felicity felt bad but didn't know what else to say. "I'll talk to you in a couple days." With a heavy heart, she moved to the door. At least he had forgiven her.

Now she would have the tougher job of facing her parents.

20

_J_ude trudged up the steps to his front door and let himself inside. All he'd gotten from Felicity today was a text saying she had made it home safely. His stomach ached, even though he wasn't hungry. No, this was something much worse. Missing her was the worst thing he'd ever felt, and not knowing when he would see her again—or *if* he would see her again—made him physically ill.

He collapsed on the couch. It had been a busy day at work, but that didn't usually make him feel this tired. He wanted to reach for the phone, call her and beg her to come back. But he knew she wouldn't be settled unless she made things right with her family.

Her words echoed in the chamber of his heart. "Forgiveness." She wanted to ask them to forgive her, and she wanted him to forgive his brother.

Jude sighed as he remembered the last time they'd spoken. Sure, they had lived in the same house all through high school, and graduated together, but Brad had managed to only speak to him if absolutely necessary. Their mother would make suggestions that they go and do things together, like homecoming football games or prom, but Jude could still see the anger in his brother's eyes every time.

"God," Jude prayed now, "show me what you want me to do. I can't imagine that showing up to talk to him will make much of a difference. He's probably the same person, and he's always hated me. It's not worth the trip, is it?" Jude heard himself making excuses but heard no answers to his question. "I'm not even the one in the wrong. How can I apologize? And showing up to say he owes me an apology is just ridiculous." Still he heard nothing. He leaned over with his elbows on his knees and folded his hands together as he closed his eyes. "God, I know. It's not about his response. It's about me doing what you call me to do. I'll be completely honest and say I don't want to go. I moved here to get away, to live my own life and not have to worry about what he thought of me. But it still hurts that my own brother doesn't have anything to do with me, and maybe, just maybe, he feels the same way. God, show me what You want me to do and I'll do it. I do care about him, and I know You do too."

When Jude rose from the couch, only one thing was certain in his mind.

It was time to go home.

FELICITY STOOD AT HER PARENTS' FRONT DOOR AND WILLED herself to ring the doorbell. She had made it this far, but with the sound of her heart pounding in her ears, she trembled as she reached up and pressed the button.

Of course, they would know she was here as soon as she did that, with the video doorbell that would show a picture on their phone screens. Maybe they wouldn't let her in. She could say she tried, right?

There was no answer on the doorbell, and her heart grew heavy. What if they didn't want to see her?

It felt like an eternity before the door cracked open and her mother opened it to let her in. She didn't say a word.

"Hi, Mom." Felicity tried a smile, but it fell flat.

"Felicity," her mother said, turning and walking down the hall.

Felicity closed the door and followed her to the living room. Her father was already sitting on the couch, his arms crossed in front of him as he watched her walk in the room.

"Hey, Dad," she said, and was met with more silence. Not knowing what else to do, she sat on the couch opposite him. Her mother sat next to him, and they both stared at her.

"Well, what do you have to say for yourself?" Dad finally spoke.

Felicity took a deep breath. "I came to say I'm sorry. I know that I hurt you both, and Clay too. I saw Clay at the house."

Her mother sat up straighter and raised her eyebrows. "You did?" A faint smile played at her lips, and a look of hope twinkled in her eyes. "What did he say?"

Felicity held up a hand. "I told him I'm sorry that I

hurt him, but that we're not right for each other." She watched as her mother's look turned to disappointment and her father looked even angrier than before. "Mom and Dad, I know you like Clay. He's a nice man, and I'm sure he's wonderful at his job. But I should have ended things a long time ago. I don't love him, and if we had gotten married, we could have been amiable, but I don't want that. I'm sorry that I went along with it because I didn't want to disappoint you. I knew from the beginning you wanted me to marry him, and so I kept trying."

"So you think this is our fault." Her father stood and paced between the fireplace and the couch. "You said you're sorry, but you're blaming us."

Felicity swallowed to keep her emotions pushed down and to give herself a moment to think. "I blame all of us. You liked him a lot, and I love you enough to try and please you." That seemed to calm her father a little bit. "Dad, you love your company and you're good at running it, but you started me on a path a long time ago, and I've always been afraid to step off of it. Now, I see that my life can be different. I don't want the life that you have. It's time for me to do something on my own, to live on my own, and make my own decisions. But I don't want to do that until I have your forgiveness."

Her father stopped pacing and plopped on the couch again. "Forgiveness?" he asked.

Felicity nodded. That would be a difficult concept for him. She couldn't remember him ever asking for forgiveness—from anyone. "Yes. I'm sorry that I let you plan the wedding and let it go that far before I walked away. I know it cost a lot of money, and it was embarrassing, and I'm sorry for that. Can you forgive me?"

"I'm not worried about the money. You're right, I'm embarrassed that you would do this. And all of this is ridiculous. You and Clay are a fine pair. He is a good man, and you shouldn't have treated him that way. What you need to do is go to him now and make it right. Marry him, and let's all get on with our lives the way they're supposed to be."

Felicity's vision blurred with the tears that stung her eyes along with his words. "That's just it, Dad. This isn't how my life is supposed to be. I know that now. Letting you convince me to marry a man I didn't love wasn't right, and committing to marry him when I knew I shouldn't wasn't good. But something good has come out of it. I spent the time since I've been gone in a wonderful little town. I met people who taught me what it's like to love and support each other, and more importantly, I met Jesus."

Her dad stood again and threw his hands up in the air. "Jesus. This is what this is all about? You've gotten religious?"

"No, Dad. This is the opposite of religious. All I've ever known about Jesus is religion, thinking that showing up to church once a year got me points that would get me into heaven. But that's not it at all. I have a relationship with Him now. I have a peace and a joy that I've never known before. He made me, and He loves me, and I want to live my life for Him. Dad, He has a plan for me, and the first step in that was to come here and make things right with you."

"Things can't be right if you choose to abandon our family."

Felicity went to him and put her hand on his arm. "I'm not abandoning you. I love you, Dad." She turned. "And you too, Mom. Things haven't always been great between us, but I tried to keep the peace by doing what you wanted me to. Now it's time for me to go, and I think it's going to be good for our relationship. I don't want to walk around on eggshells with you anymore. So what if we start now? It's time for us to have a grown-up relationship."

She watched their faces as they moved from anger to disappointment. Silently, she prayed for them that God would soften their hearts and help them to understand.

21

Jude climbed out of the car and thanked the driver. It had all happened so fast that now he couldn't believe he was standing here. He couldn't remember when he had asked off work, so when he said it was a family situation, they gave him the time without a second thought. After that, it was a flight to Kentucky and a car from the airport and now he was in front of his parents' house.

Last he'd heard, Brad lived just down the street and he spent a lot of time with his parents. It would be easy for Mom to tell Jude where he was. But first things first. It was a good thing he was a doctor because he was about to give his mom a heart attack.

He rang the doorbell and stood back. As strange as it felt to be back here, it was even stranger to ring the bell at the home he grew up in.

The door opened slowly at first, then flew open wide as he heard his mom gasp. "Jude!" she shouted.

Jude smiled but had to catch himself as she came

forward and threw her arms around him. "Hi, Mom. Surprise."

"Surprise?" she said, standing back to look at him as if she still wasn't sure he was really there. "This is a miracle. Why didn't you tell me you were coming?"

"It was a last-minute decision. I just decided it was time."

His mom pulled him in the house and shut the door behind him. She hugged him again and then looked him over from head to toe. She narrowed her eyes. "Just now you decided?" She tapped an index finger on her lips and then gasped again. "You've met someone."

Jude's cheeks grew hot. How could she tell that from looking at him? "Actually, I have. She's wonderful, Mom. I didn't even know I wanted to find someone, but she's it. But that's not why I'm here."

Mom grabbed the doorknob and threw the door open again, looking left and right. "Where is she?"

Jude laughed, and then sadness grew in his chest. "She's not with me, Mom." Oh, how he wished she was.

"Well, why not? You finally come home after all these years, you tell me you've met someone, and she didn't even come with you?"

"I told you, that's not what this is about. Mom, can we sit down to talk, please?"

Her eyes grew wide. "Yes, yes, come in. I'm sorry, I'm just in shock. Your father is out running an errand. He'll be back in a little while. Have you…have you talked to your brother?"

Jude motioned to the kitchen. "Mom, come on please. Let's sit."

She moved quickly into the kitchen and took a seat at the kitchen table. "Do you want something to drink? Are you hungry?"

"No, I'm fine, Mom."

"All right, then tell me why you're here. I'm thrilled to see you, but I know you didn't just come without a reason."

Jude folded his hands on the table in front of him and prayed that God would help him with the words. "It's about Brad. We haven't spoken in years. You don't know the whole story, but it doesn't matter. Things were bad between us in high school, and I'm here because it's time to forgive each other and move on."

Mom's eyes filled with tears as she breathed a huge sigh of relief. "Oh, son, you don't know how long I've waited to hear that. I hoped it would come from Brad. You're right, I don't know the whole story, but I've always believed that he was the one who started it. It broke my heart when you left for Colorado. Not because I didn't want you to go somewhere, but because I felt like you were running away from him."

Jude nodded. "I didn't handle it well, but I was young and I thought distance was the best thing. Now I can see that distance has only made it worse. I don't know if he wants to talk to me, but I have to try."

"Yes, I think you might be surprised."

"Really? Why?" Jude narrowed his eyes.

"You should talk to him."

"That's why I'm here."

"Well then you're just in time." Mom stood and made

her way to the door, looking through the glass window beside it. "He's walking up the driveway."

Jude had asked hundreds of patients where the pain was, and now he clutched his chest wondering if this is what it felt like when people complained of chest pain. His heart beat at an unnatural rhythm and his palms were wet. He blinked rapidly as he stood, almost wishing he could find a place to hide. The miles of the flight and drive hadn't prepared him as well as he had hoped. Clearing his throat, he clasped his hands in front of him as Mom opened the door.

"Hi, Brad," Mom said, keeping her voice even. Jude couldn't see them, but could hear from the front door. "There's someone here I want you to see."

Jude waited, listening to his heart pound in his ears, drowning out the footsteps coming into the kitchen. Brad appeared and stopped in the doorway when their eyes met.

"Hey," Jude said.

Brad seemed unable to speak at first. There were several beats of silence before he said, "Jude."

"I know it's been a long time."

Brad nodded, but the next words out of his mouth gave Jude a tiny ray of hope. "Too long."

"Why don't you two boys go in the living room and talk. I'm going to make some coffee, and I think I have some leftover pie. I'll warm it up."

Jude didn't look at Brad as they both moved into the other room. Jude had practiced what he would say, but now the words seemed far away. Only God could help him now.

"Brad, I came here to talk to you. I've waited too long to do it, but I'm here now."

"Wait." Brad held up a hand. "I think I'm the one who needs to start. I was a terrible brother. I've known it for a long time, but I've never had to the guts to call you up and say it. You coming here…" He paused and cleared his throat, clearly pushing down emotions that had been building for years. "You're the real man, Jude. You had the strength to tell me no all those years ago, even when I put you down and treated you terribly. If you had let me cheat off of you, I would have stayed the spoiled teenager that I was."

Jude sat frozen on the couch. Was his brother really saying these things?

Brad continued. "I thought I would die when I had to retake that class over the summer. But that's when I finally learned to work hard for something that I wanted. I'm not as smart as you, it never came as easily for me, but I learned to work with what I had. I have a good job now, a house, and I'm dating a woman I think I'm really falling for. The truth is, if I had skated through that class all those years ago, I don't think I would be who I am." He dropped his gaze to the floor. "Too bad I've never been man enough to tell you that. The hardest words to say are I'm sorry, and I should have said them a long time ago. I'm sorry, Jude."

Jude pressed his hands to his knees, trying to take it all in. Slowly, he nodded as he knew what he needed to say. "I've already forgiven you, Brad. It took me a long time, and I'm sorry it did. We both grew up in church and knew right from wrong, but this Christmas I've learned what it means to truly follow Jesus. And if Jesus can forgive me, and everyone in the world, for my sins, I can forgive you for this too."

Jude stood and moved toward his brother. The boy he had grown up with was gone. This was a man who was very different. Jude hated all the years they had lost but hoped this could be the beginning of a different relationship with him. Without a word, Brad stood and the two men embraced. It wasn't a long hug, but it was enough to show that they were ready to put the past behind them.

"Here we are now." Mom came in, carrying two plates of pie. She set them on the table before she wiped at her eyes. "I never thought I would see this sight, but I've prayed for it." She hugged Brad and then Jude. "I love you both, very much." She sniffed once more. "Now, there's coffee in the kitchen if you want it."

Brad and Jude moved to the kitchen and fixed two cups of coffee. As they did, they spoke about their work and their lives. The words tumbled out at a speed of desperation as they worked to learn all they had missed.

When they settled back in on the couch in the living room with coffee and pie, Mom spoke up. "Now, Jude, tell me about this girl."

22

Felicity walked through the upstairs guest bedroom of her parents' house and tripped over her suitcase. She cried out and then sat on the bed, rubbing her sore toe.

"I can't live like this much longer," she said out loud to no one. She knew she needed to talk to the only one who could hear her. "God," she started, "I came here to make things right with my parents, and with Clay. And now he's living in my house, and I'm stuck here with my parents, who don't quite know what to think of me." She sighed. "I'm not sure what I pictured, but this wasn't it. I did the only thing I knew I was supposed to do. So now what?" She held her palms toward the ceiling and shrugged, hoping for an answer.

Nothing was written on the ceiling that she stared up at. "God, I gave You my life, and I meant it. I want to do whatever it is You have for me. I spent too many years just doing what people expected of me, and I never felt like what I did mattered. But I know You have a plan and a purpose for me. Please show me, God." She squeezed her eyes shut and sat in silence. She wanted to envision a future with a job that God had for her and a place to live that wasn't her parents' guest room.

The only thing she could think about was Jude.

Her eyes filled with tears as she thought of the man who was the first person who had ever listened to her and understood her. She missed him with all of her being.

"God," she said, emotion filling her throat and making it hard for the words to come out. "I don't know what I want to do with my life, or what You have for me. All I know is, I want to be with Jude. We both chose to follow You, but, God, could we please follow You together?"

The peace and joy that she had felt the first time she prayed was always with her, but now it washed over her like a flood. She didn't know what was going to happen, but she didn't have to worry. God would provide for her, and He had a good plan for her.

And in her heart she knew that Jude was her future.

JUDE PUT HIS HAND TO HIS HEAD AS HE STEPPED INTO THE airport. He hadn't flown much in his life, and now he knew he didn't like it. Did everyone feel dizzy when they stepped off a plane?

Still, he would do it all again to be where he was now. He whispered the quiet prayer that he hadn't stopped praying since a few days ago in his mom's living room. "Thank you."

God had changed his life, and now he had a brother

again. He and Brad had talked practically non-stop for two days. They had missed too much to waste another second. Jude thanked God for the chance to talk to his brother about Jesus. Like Jude, he had been going to church and trying to make sense of his faith. After praying together—another miracle in itself—Brad and Jude were not only biological brothers, but true brothers in Christ.

As Jude made his way to baggage claim, he prayed in his mind about his next steps. *God, I never planned for this. After talking to my brother, it seems strange to go back to Freedom and live alone, but I love my work, and now I've fallen for the people and the town there.*

He had fallen for someone else too, and he prayed without ceasing about that. *God, please give me a future with Felicity.*

It took much longer than he hoped for him to get his bags and rent a car, and he was anxious to get going. And hopeful that the Lord had prepared a way for him.

23

Felicity sat at the desk she had worked at since she graduated from college. There were a few pictures and some knickknacks—just a few things that said this was her space.

But the Felicity who had put those things there wasn't the same person she was anymore. She packed up a few things, but most of them went into the garbage. That life was behind her, and it was time to move on. As she put a picture of herself and Clay into the bag, she prayed that God would lead him to Jesus and give him a wife that would be a perfect fit for him, and she let him go.

When the desk held none of her personal items anymore, she stood and picked up her purse. The conversation with her dad had been hard, but she knew it was the right thing to do when she told him she was quitting.

"What will you do?" he asked, his voice tense.

"I don't know yet. But I know I need to move on. I love you, Dad. From now on I won't be your employee. I'll just be your daughter."

Her stomach knotted as she walked out of the office and down the hall to the elevator. It was true that she didn't know what she was going to do. But over the past few days, she had packed up most her things from the house. Clay wanted to stay, and she didn't want the house. Her parents had worked out an agreement with him. She didn't know the details, but it didn't matter to her. They could sell it to him, rent it to him, or give it to him. It wasn't ever really hers.

Now that was decided, it left her with a decision to make. Where was she going to go? More than anything, she wanted to load up her car and drive to Freedom and never look back. But she and Jude hadn't talked about that. She couldn't move somewhere just for a guy, could she? No, she would only move somewhere if she knew for sure that was what God wanted her to do.

So far, God hadn't given her any answers for that. With no job prospects in Colorado, besides working part-time at Wick and Sarcasm, it didn't seem like a wise decision. She had even glanced at job listings in the area, but nothing seemed right for her. As she carried the small box of her belongings out of the elevator and into the lobby, she let out a sigh. Maybe soon she would have an answer. Today she could only do what she knew she was supposed to do, and that was to clean out her desk and move on.

When she reached the lobby, she stopped and set the box on the counter to hand the woman at the front her badge to scan in the building. She could have kept it—her dad wouldn't say anything—but if she was coming to visit him, she wanted it to be a visit, and she could stop at the desk and say she was there to see her father. She smiled at the thought of it. Visiting her dad at work might be nice when she wasn't his employee.

She picked up her box and turned, but before she took a step, she heard a voice.

"You know, you shouldn't be lifting that much weight on your wrist. It might not heal properly."

Felicity gasped and practically dropped the box on the floor. "Jude," she said, rushing to him and wrapping her arms around his neck.

He enveloped her in his arms, and she never wanted to let go.

"Jude," she repeated. "What are you doing here? I thought you were in Freedom."

He pushed back and held her shoulders as he looked her in the eyes. "No, actually, I've been in Kentucky."

Felicity put her fingertips to her mouth as she gasped. "You have? Your brother?" she asked.

He nodded. "You were right. I didn't want to go, but I prayed about it, and God said it was time." He cleared his throat, and Felicity thought she saw tears in his eyes before he blinked them away. "It was the best decision. I wasted so much time not going to him."

"So you told him you forgave him?" Felicity asked.

"He apologized before I could say anything. Said I was the bigger man to come to him, but he was the one with something to be sorry about."

"Oh, Jude, that's wonderful. You got your brother back."

"I did," he said. "I never thought that would happen. I have to give God all the credit for that. And you. Felicity, I never would have gone if you hadn't said something. Thank you for not being quiet. You were right, and I hope you always speak up for what you think is right."

She shook her head as tears filled her own eyes. "You don't know how good it is to hear you say that. All my life I've just followed what people told me to do. Things are different now, and I'm ready to move on. I won't stay quiet anymore."

"There's something else I need to say." Jude blinked rapidly before he spoke again. "I was afraid when you left. It tore me up inside because I knew how badly I would miss you. It's more than that, though. I was afraid I wouldn't see you again."

"Jude, I wouldn't let that happen."

"I know that now. Looking in your eyes, I can see that we could never stay apart for long. It's just that I'm used to people getting what they want from me and then walking away."

Felicity put her hands in his and ran her thumb over his fingers. "Like your brother?"

"Like my brother. Like other people who wanted me to help them study for a test, or write a paper, then they went back to their popular friends and never spoke to me again. I loved spending Christmas with you in Freedom. I fell in love with the town and the Christmas season more than I ever have, and I was grateful for that. I knew I would be grateful for it, even after you left. Because I was sure after Christmas that you would be gone. We would have Christmas, and then you would go back to live your own life."

"I could never do that. Once I met you and got to know the town, I knew it was the only place I wanted to be. Not just in Freedom, but with you."

He looked into her eyes and knew she meant every word. "I love you," he said, unable to keep the words inside anymore. "I love your eyes and your smile and the way you walk into a room and the energy changes. You go after what you want and you bring all the light of your life into everything you do."

Felicity shook her head and laughed. "Jude, don't you see? Everything you love about me is because of you. I wasn't that girl before. I was quiet and nervous and afraid of doing or saying the wrong thing all the time. When I came to Freedom, I decided it was time to be someone new, but I was still scared. Then you said yes to spending time with me. I knew it was just for fun, but having you by my side gave me the confidence to just try. I love you, Jude. You gave me the freedom to be myself, and in doing so, you helped me find who I really am. And who I am loves you."

Jude dropped her hands and cupped her face in both of his hands. He leaned close and savored every bit of this moment with her. He took a quick breath before closing the distance between them.

When their lips met, Felicity knew it was forever. He kissed her slowly, as if he had the rest of his life to kiss her. And she was sure he did.

He stepped back as if he remembered that they were in an office building. Felicity giggled as she put a hand to her mouth. Glancing behind her, she saw that the receptionist seemed to be trying not to stare. "Want to get out of here?" she asked.

"Sure," he said, stepping to pick up the box she had dropped on the floor. "Where do you want to go?"

"Anywhere, as long as it's with you."

elicity walked slowly to her car, pulling her suitcase behind her. Keeping her eyes on what was in front, she didn't bother to glance over her shoulder.

"Here, let me take that for you," Jude said, reaching for the bag. He opened the trunk and set it beside his.

"Good morning," Felicity said, stepping close to give him a kiss. "How was the hotel?"

Jude shrugged. "I barely noticed it. All I could think about was waking up this morning and getting to see you."

"I hope you're not too tired to drive." Felicity covered a yawn. "I know we stayed up too late talking."

Jude laughed. "Most people wouldn't think I was capable of talking that much."

She put her arms around his neck, and he moved his hands to her hips. When he looked her in the eyes, she said, "Maybe not, but I know you. The real you."

"And I know the real you." He pressed a kiss to her lips. "We better get going."

Felicity walked to the passenger side of her car, and Jude opened the door for her. She watched as he walked in front of the car, thinking he was the most handsome man she'd ever seen.

As Jude backed the car out of the driveway, Felicity looked at her parents' house one last time.

"Will you and your parents be okay?"

Felicity sighed. "I hope so. No, I won't say that. I believe we will be one day, but it's going to take some time. A lot of change happened fast, and for the first time in my life, they weren't part of the decision. I think it will be good for us though. The distance might help. I plan to call them regularly, and I hope they will come visit. I would love for them to see Freedom, but I pray that one day they will know Jesus."

Jude laced his fingers through hers. "I will pray for that too."

As they turned toward the interstate, Felicity let her thoughts run out loud. "A few weeks ago, I made this same drive, and now, nothing could be more different." She looked over at Jude. "When I jumped in my car at the country club and drove away, I thought I was running away. I needed to get out of there, as far away as I could. I didn't know that I was running to something. I'd never known true freedom." She laughed. "I didn't know it was a town in Colorado."

Jude lifted her hand to his lips and kissed her fingers. "I don't want to think about what my life would be if you hadn't come. Jesus is the one who saved me, but He used you to do it."

Felicity smiled as they drove toward Freedom. "I thought I was running away, but I was running to you."

"I hope you always do."

She leaned over and kissed his cheek, making sure he kept his eyes on the road.

"Sweetie," Jude said, "let's go home."

EPILOGUE

Felicity stared at herself in the mirror. The dress was everything she could have wanted. The fitted lace bodice with a skirt that fell just to the floor was classic but simple, and the moment she'd seen it on the rack, she'd known it was hers. She fingered her long hair in soft curls that cascaded over her shoulders and down her back.

"Are you ready?" Ashley asked, holding her bouquet in front of her.

Felicity nodded. "I think so."

"You look perfect." Ashley gave her a side hug, careful not to mess up her hair. The two women had gotten even closer over the months since Felicity moved to Freedom for good. "You're the best looking business manager I've ever seen."

Felicity laughed. "It's a good thing you hired me and recommended me to others in town. Otherwise, I wouldn't be able to have this wedding. Or live in Freedom. I never would have guessed that I would start my own business helping others run their companies."

"I'm the lucky one. You have changed my business, and others in town too. Even Jude's cabin stays booked year 'round because of you promoting it."

"I know. I couldn't even get it for our honeymoon this week." She laughed.

"No, you don't want that anyway. You and Jude deserve a break. He's worked every holiday at the hospital and never takes a vacation. This one was worth the wait."

Felicity's cheeks were hot, and she pressed her hand to her face to hide the color. "I hope so."

"You bet it will be. Now, you just enjoy today, and you take your whole week away, then you can come back ready to work."

"You got it."

The door opened and her dad stuck his head in. "It's time." He gave her a smile, and the skin around his eyes crinkled. "You look wonderful, Felicity."

"Thanks, Dad. It means so much to me for you to be here."

"I wouldn't miss it," he said.

Felicity blinked away the tears. They had been through a rough patch, and they still had a ways to go. Talking on the phone every week had been good for them, and Felicity almost couldn't believe it when they agreed to come to her wedding. She didn't ask them to pay for anything, but her dad had given them a small sum to put toward the event. They hadn't given any other input and allowed Felicity to plan the wedding however she wanted.

Ashley handed her the bouquet, and as she moved through the door with her dad, she whispered a prayer of thanks to God for the work He was doing in their lives. And she prayed that He wouldn't stop working on her parents.

———

Jude would never have imagined today. Marrying the woman who had changed his life for the better would have been enough, that was for sure, but even more than that, he was blown away by his brother standing next to him as they walked into the church. Just before they stepped through the door into the sanctuary, Brad turned to him and hugged him.

"Thank you for being here," Jude said.

"Thanks for asking me. I'm so proud to stand up with you today, but I know I'm not the best man. You are, Jude."

Jude grinned. "I'll be happy to be the best man when you propose to Courtney."

Brad blushed. "I already bought the ring."

"Don't wait, man. Life is exciting. You just have to go out there and live it."

Brad nodded, then turned and followed the pastor in through the door.

Jude moved to his spot and watched as his parents and Felicity's mother were led to their seats. So much had changed in the year since he first met her. When they moved back to Freedom at the beginning of the year, he could hardly wait to propose. He lasted until Valentine's Day. When she said yes, he knew she would want to celebrate their new life together at Christmastime. Now he could see the snow falling out the window against the backdrop of the Christmas wreaths and bows in the church.

Everything else was a blur. He didn't care about the music they played or what type of flowers they picked. He didn't notice anything else, until the guests rose and the back doors opened and he looked for the most beautiful woman he'd ever known. Inside and out.

He was caught up in her eyes as she came and stood before him. He heard the voices around him but only saw her. When he took her hand, he was grateful he paid enough attention to say "I do" and repeat the vows. Finally, the preacher was saying the only words he cared about. "I pronounce you husband and wife."

He smiled at her. They had done it. Saying yes to Christmas last year had led them here. Jude took her in his arms and kissed her. She was his wife and he never had to leave her side again.

"I love you," he whispered.

"I love you, too," she replied.

The reception went off without a hitch. They danced, they ate cake, and their friends and family celebrated with them.

When it was time to leave, Jude took Felicity's hand and lifted it to his lips and gently kissed her fingers. "Are you ready to go?"

"I am. Are you ready for the rest of our lives?"

Jude took a breath and let it out in a happy sigh. "Felicity, when I first met you, I knew I needed to say yes to you and it would change my life. So I say yes. Yes to you and yes to forever."

ABOUT THE AUTHOR

Hannah Jo Abbott is not just a writer, but a wife, a mom of four, a homeschool teacher, a daughter, a sister, and a friend. She loves writing stories about life, love, and the grace of God. She finds inspiration and encouragement from reading the stories others share. Hannah lives with her husband and children in Sweet Home Alabama.

For updates on her writing and to receive a FREE novella, sign up for Hannah Jo's newsletters at www.hannahjoabbott.com

facebook.com/hjabooks

instagram.com/hannahjoabbottwriter

ALSO BY HANNAH JO ABBOTT

Whispering Oaks Ranch Series:

Hope for the Cowboy

Courage for the Cowboy

Match for the Cowboy

Sweet Home Billionaire Series:

Small Town Billionaire

Hometown Billionaire

Downtown Billionaire

Faith and Love Series:

Walk with Me

Dream with me

Stay with Me

Come with Me

Love Off Limits Series:

Her Best Friend

Her Roommate's Brother

Her Brother's Best Friend

His Daughter's Teacher

Her Sister's Ex

Heroes of Freedom Ridge Series:

Stranded with The Hero

Trusting The Hero

Billionaire for Christmas Series:

Billionaire Under the Mistletoe

Billionaire at The Christmas Inn